I0630105

My Younger Lover

Shelley Munro

My Younger Lover

Copyright © 2016 by Shelley Munro

Print ISBN: 978-1-99-115878-9
Digital ISBN: 978-0-473-34713-0

Editor: Mary Moran

Cover: Kim Killion

This book is a work of fiction. The names, characters, places, and incidents are products of the writer's imagination or have been used fictitiously and are not to be construed as real. Any resemblance to persons, living or dead, actual events, locales, or organizations is entirely coincidental.

All rights reserved. No portion of this book may be reproduced, scanned, or distributed in any manner without prior written permission from the author, except in the case of a brief quotation embodied in critical articles and reviews.

Munro Press, New Zealand.

First Munro Press electronic publication February 2016

First Munro Press print publication September 2022

For Paul.

Introduction

Never let an opportunity pass by...

F eline shifter Lisa Jordan lost her husband two years ago and now it's time to start living again. At the Middlemarch Singles Ball, she's attracted to a sexy shifter, but his identity comes as a huge shock. Big, big shock since the man she's ogling is one she knew as a teenager.

Sam Mitchell has harbored a crush on Lisa for years. A relationship was impossible then, but now he's eager to stake his claim. A few dances turn into a one-night stand full of exciting, satisfying sex. Sam wants more, but first he'll need to persuade Lisa to his way of thinking.

Back at home in Christchurch, Lisa's life takes a different turn when she attracts the attention of a mystery stalker. Juggling her safety and a romance with the gorgeous Sam is certainly spicing up her life. If only she lives to enjoy the rewards.

Note to Readers

W elcome to the second book in my **Middlemarch Shifters** series. *My Younger Lover* started life as a short story called *Lightning Strikes Twice*. I've always liked Lisa and Sam, the main characters, and decided they deserved better than a short 7000-word romance. After pondering for a few weeks, I came up with a suspense plot to weave through their romance. I hope you enjoy Lisa and Sam's journey as much as I enjoyed writing it.

Happy reading,
Shelley

Chapter 1

The Game

Outskirts Christchurch, New Zealand

"I've found one." James Silcock, advertising bigwig, watched his twin closely, his breath easing out at his brother's flicker of interest—immediately controlled, but a reaction, nonetheless.

Tyler Silcock ambled over to the picture window to peer outside. He remained silent, staring at the lights of the suburbs that stretched toward the sea.

"Looking for paparazzi? You won't find any around here, not even for a famous mystery author like you," James teased his brother.

Tyler snorted and wheeled away from the view to face him. "Another game?"

"If you agree Lisa is worthy."

Tyler dropped into a comfortable leather chair and stretched, lifting his arms, elongating his torso like a pampered cat. It was like staring into a mirror. Same features. Same hazel eyes. Same dimple. These days Tyler wore his chocolate-brown hair short, yet still long enough to express his individuality. At present, his charcoal-gray suit jacket gaped open, and as James watched, his twin tugged at his red tie, loosening the knot for greater comfort. As usual, he'd arrived without fanfare and worn a disguise—now discarded—to prevent recognition by friends and acquaintances. By fans. Maybe he needed the game as much as James did—a sense of challenge and renewed purpose instead of the normal day-to-day drudgery.

"Want a drink?"

"Yeah. I could do with one after mother's lectures. My ears are still ringing from her tirade last night. I couldn't wait to complete my publicity for the new book and leave Auckland. She rang Allison and plunged into full matchmaking mode."

James chuckled as he wandered to a sideboard and pulled a decanter of brandy from a cupboard with a pearl-inset design. Now that Allison knew of Tyler's arrival back in New Zealand from the US, she'd spread the word. No wonder his twin had turned up here. "At least you managed to escape to Christchurch. We have miles between us and Mother." He poured two measures of brandy into crystal balloon snifters and handed one to his brother. "I wish I could've seen the look on your face."

Tyler grunted. "I know I'd witness unholy delight on yours. I wondered why you'd decided to move south. Now I understand."

"It's good to see you. Glad you had time to visit me." James dropped onto a black leather chair that faced his twin and sipped his brandy, waiting for Tyler to make the next move. "How long are you staying?"

"Tell me about this woman." Tyler tapped his forefinger against the sparkling surface of his snifter.

"She's a graphic designer and runs her own business. Her husband died a couple of years ago, and as far as I know, there's no man in her life. She's tall. Great figure. A sense of humor. Hard worker."

"Have you slept with her?"

Ah, Tyler sounded interested. He hadn't asked about her hair or eyes yet. A good sign. "Not yet. I met her through work at a design conference."

"She intelligent?"

"She'd make a worthy adversary."

"What about family? Friends? Anyone to get in our way?"

"Her husband was an only child. Lisa's family lives in Dunedin and some farther south in a country town called Middlemarch. She has gone to visit in Middlemarch this weekend. She told me when we ran into each other in the city center. We had coffee together."

"Have you done any research? Photos?"

James hid a victorious smile as he set his brandy on a kauri coffee table and stood. He padded across the thick carpet toward his home office, taking pleasure in the soft luxury of the woolen pile. A new purchase and well worth the expense. In his office, he strode behind his desk and opened a drawer. With a manila folder in hand, he returned to his brother.

He waited while Tyler removed his jacket, then handed over the folder and returned to his seat. He pictured Lisa in his mind, her wide smile, her glittering eyes and her trim, sexy legs encased in stockings. At least, he hoped they were stockings. Much sexier. She'd been relaxed and pleased to see him, accepting his offer of a quick coffee without hesitation.

As he sipped his brandy, he turned his attention to Tyler, wanting to read his reactions to the information he'd acquired to date. Excitement simmered in his belly, but he fought the restless urge he had to pace. He didn't want Tyler to know how much this meant to him, how much he needed a new challenge and a contest with his brother for a woman would be just the thing to enliven his dull life and drag him from his rut.

James noticed his fingers had turned white from holding his glass too tightly. He eased his grip and continued to study Tyler as he turned the pages. He saw the moment Tyler got to the candid pictures, the photos he'd so painstakingly snapped while he followed Lisa during her day.

"You said she's attractive. You're wrong. She's beautiful. What color are her eyes?"

"Blue. She has clear tropical sea-blue eyes. They're stunning with her black hair."

"Does she wear contacts?"

"I don't think so, but we could find out during a game." James held his breath, waiting for his brother's decision. At three minutes older than him, Tyler usually took the lead. It was important to him that Tyler agree to Lisa as their third player in this delicious game of cat and mouse.

"You've thought of everything." Tyler glanced up with a warm smile. "You've done well. When does she return from Middlemarch?"

"Sunday evening. She has a client meeting at nine on Monday morning."

"Did you ask her out?"

"I did. We have a dinner date on Wednesday."

"Perfect. When and where? I should get my manuscript off to my editor tomorrow. That will leave me plenty of time to play before I start my next mystery. I'll book a table at the same restaurant, so I can observe. A new disguise, I think."

James grinned, his restlessness dispersing now that Tyler had agreed. "A side bet to make things interesting?"

Tyler's hazel eyes gleamed. "First-stage bet—ten thousand for the one who manages to make her noticeably edgy first. Second-stage bet—another ten to the one she turns to once she becomes frightened. And third-stage bet—ten thousand to the first one who gets her in bed. Would that work?"

James scratched his chin and considered the bet. "No physical harm. We're just scaring her."

Tyler gave a nod. "Agreed."

"Looks as if we have a new game. A toast?"

"To the beautiful Lisa," Tyler said and raised his glass.

James lifted his own glass and clicked it against Tyler's goblet. "To Lisa and our new game."

Inaugural Singles Ball, Middlemarch, New Zealand

"You need a man. Do you see anyone tempting? Someone sexy for a naughty fling."

"I don't want a man. And I don't need a one-night stand." Lisa Jordan scanned the packed marquee while trying not to dwell on her sister's outrageous suggestion. The band came to the end of a lively Beatles tune and shifted into a slow ballad. "And, I have met someone."

"You have?" Janice quirked an eyebrow, curiosity simmering off her in waves. Older than Lisa by three years, she took her sisterly duties seriously. Too seriously.

Lisa ignored the silent demand for more information as they both watched friends and neighbors having a good time from the table she, Janice and Janice's husband Craig had claimed on their arrival. Craig had slipped off to gossip with some of his friends at the bar, leaving them alone.

Janice picked up her glass, took a quick sip, then wriggled it in front of Lisa's nose. "Where? Who? Don't make me beat the answers out of you."

Lisa sighed and sampled her white wine while debating her response. She should've known mentioning James was a mistake. "I met him at the design conference I attended

11

and we ran into each other again yesterday. His name is James Silcock, and he seems very nice. He asked me out to dinner."

"Did you accept?"

Lisa scowled. "I did. Not that it's any of your business."

"Good for you, but I still say you need a fling. Think of it as a kick-start into the dating game. Things have changed since you last dated."

"I'm not that old."

"Good." Janice's smirk held a trace of wickedness. Her blue eyes twinkled in echo of her mindset. "I was beginning to wonder. See, even some of the council members are dancing, and they're much older than you. You can have some fun."

Lisa followed her sister's line of sight and saw Sid Blackburn waltzing with Valerie McClintock. Both were members of the ruling Feline Council that had organized this function. A success. They must be pleased.

Groups of men and women laughed and chatted and danced together on the makeshift grass dancefloor. The sweet scent of carnations and roses drifted from the floral arrangement on their table. She caught a whiff of spicy perfume with amber and patchouli undertones as a woman wearing a tight black dress with a slit up the thigh sashayed past, her left hand encased in Leo Mitchell's right.

At least Lisa thought it was Leo. They headed for the dance floor and once there, claimed a spot to sway together.

Rumor said the Middlemarch elders hoped the ball would attract women to the district. They wanted the female sex to distract the male feline shifters from mischief. If the gossip ran true, the plan was working because everywhere she turned, smiles and flirtation abounded.

Her right foot tapped in rhythm with the band. David had loved to dance. A pang shot through her—bittersweet rather than agonized as it had once been.

Sweetheart, you have to move on. Janice is right—you do need a fling.

Lisa forced a smile as she continued scrutinizing the area, searching for childhood friends and familiar faces. David's ghostly voice had become increasingly pushy, urging her to move on after his unexpected illness and death. And she would—in her own time. She had a dinner date. A new start.

Why do I need a fling? I have the vibe you bought me. It works perfectly well. Besides one-night stands are tacky.

David's sexy chuckle echoed through her mind. *But they feel good. Remember how we met?*

Oh yeah. She remembered. Heat flooded her cheeks as she recalled leaving the party two hours after initial introductions. They'd gone straight to her apartment and spent the rest of the weekend in bed. Their one-night stand had led to love and marriage. Lisa scowled. Point taken, but lightning never strikes in the same place twice.

A husky, masculine laugh snared her attention, and she let her gaze drift in that direction. A muscular body clad from head to foot in black. Her eyes scanned his length and came to rest on a tight butt. A tingle sprang to life, sinking downward in time with her gaze to settle between her thighs.

She shifted her weight, aware of her blue dress and lacy panties clinging to her skin. "Wow, I'd like to sink my teeth into his butt. Clothing optional." The words popped out of her mouth unbidden and she gasped in consternation.

The ghost of David sniggered along with Janice.

"I could introduce you." A mischievous note entered Janice's voice, alerting Lisa to a pitfall.

"He's married. There's something wrong with him. That look on your face is a giveaway. His rear end is false advertising. He's old with buckteeth and dyed hair. A toupee."

"The front view is just as sexy," Janice reassured her.

The man turned and Lisa slapped her hand over her open mouth, but not before an *eep* of shock escaped. "Sam Mitchell. Oh my god, I feel like a dirty old woman."

"He's grown up fine."

"Not for me," Lisa said firmly while she ordered her mutinous body to get a grip. Sam and his tantalizing butt fell into forbidden territory. "I used to babysit Sam and his sisters before the family moved to Christchurch."

"Which makes you not much older," her sister pointed out. "What are a few years if you're flat on a mattress in the dark?"

Heat bloomed in her face. "Janice!"

"I loved David too, but he's been gone for almost two years. It's time for you to have some fun."

Janice is right, sweetheart. You need to spread your wings and soar again. Brush off your widow's weeds and fly like a butterfly in your sexy blue dress.

"He's heading this direction." Janice lifted a hand in a wave, and seconds later, he stood in front of them.

Seated, she felt at a disadvantage, so she stood to greet Sam.

Tall—at least six inches taller than she—with short black hair, strong features, dominated by his compelling sea-green gaze, broad shoulders and... Oh boy. *Eyes front. No. Higher!* He was *not* a prize bull for purchase. She did not need to study anything apart from his face and his sexy eyes.

Lisa smiled and concentrated on holding her ground. She'd been mistaken. There was nothing wrong with his front view. One glance at his sinful body and her feline sat up and purred approval. Lisa agreed wholeheartedly with her feline's assessment. Sam... He stole her breath and made her mind focus on sex and those tingly good feelings that came with horizontal togetherness. Her conscience told her she'd accepted a date with another man, but the thought seeped away when faced with Sam.

"Lisa, it's great to see you. Janice told me you were coming to the Singles Ball. You look just the same."

"You're taller."

Janice snickered and another blush swept into Lisa's cheeks. Mortified, she cast about her mind for something to say that wouldn't make her sound idiotic.

Sam's casual stance shrieked of confidence, a man sure of his place in the world. "I was sixteen when you last saw me. I have grown since then. Come and dance." He took possession of her hand and tugged.

"Wouldn't you prefer to dance with someone your own age?"

A flash of something undecipherable flickered across his face, but his smile never faltered. "I'm twenty-five. Old enough to choose my dance partners."

"And I'm thirty-two," Lisa protested.

"For goodness' sake, dance with the man," Janice said. "You might even enjoy yourself."

That was the problem. From the instant she'd caught sight of him her hormones had jumped to attention and snapped a salute, her mind focusing on sin with Sam instead of sparing a thought for James and her upcoming date. Her stomach flipped in a good way and the feline part of her psyche dwelled on closer contact. Touching. Lots of touching. Stroking. Petting. Purring.

She wanted Sam with an intensity she hadn't felt since David's death. It was exhilarating and scary and inappropriate as hell. At her age, she should know better. She didn't get involved with two men at once. *She didn't.*

Sam guided Lisa onto the dance floor, not daring to release her trembling hand because he suspected she'd run. His feline stirred, taut and edgy with the need to act. Take control. He'd had a crush on Lisa since age ten. It had taken him a while to get his head around his unwavering desire for her, but he'd finally recognized his feline nature speaking. Lisa was his mate.

And tonight was the night.

He intended to make his move and, if he were lucky, he'd get her into his bed and keep her there. She was as skittish as a wild cat, her unusual blue eyes holding wariness. She'd restrained her black hair in a tight knot at her nape, and he couldn't wait to release the pins and combs and watch the heavy mass tumble down her back. The sole plus for her bound hair was that it allowed him to appreciate the naked expanse of her back, the curve of her shoulders and neck left bare by her halter-neck dress. Soon he'd touch her golden skin and test it for softness and smoothness. He wanted to make her purr, preferably once he got her out of her tight blue dress.

Glad of the crush and the melodic ballad, he guided her into a dark corner and took her in his arms. Sweet and curvy with an underlying sexiness, her smile laced with mischief, or at least it used to be before her husband died. He wanted her bad.

"You smell good." And her skin felt warm and silky beneath his fingertips. He trailed his fingers over her naked back again, just because he could.

"So do you." Her muffled voice barely reached him, but he could smell her arousal, the floral and musky scent of her boosting his hopes. A single night wasn't enough. He intended to have her future.

A mate.

"Are you looking for a husband?"

Her head jerked up and she stared at him. She caught her bottom lip between her teeth. "No, but I get...lonely sometimes."

"You miss sex?" Hell, this conversation couldn't have gone better if he'd scripted the words himself. He hadn't expected her to answer his question.

She swallowed but monitored his reaction. He let his interest loose, knowing it would blaze in his eyes, stamp the rest of his features. If she agreed, he didn't want any misunderstandings. He intended to fuck her tonight and into the small hours of the morning until they were both sated and exhausted.

After a long pause, she nodded, a tiny shudder working through her tense muscles. "Yes, I miss having a man in my bed."

"I didn't think you'd admit it."

A laugh burst from her. "Me neither. I'm too old to discuss sex with you."

"But I'm taller," he reminded her.

She chuckled, a sultry sound that grabbed his nuts and twisted. Sam drew her even closer, letting her brush against his erection. It wouldn't hurt her to experience the physical proof of his attraction. "I'm all grown up. I know about sex."

Something shifted in her then. She stiffened, and he knew she saw him as a mature man. An equal.

"But are you good at it?"

"You'll have to let me know." The last of the tension residing in his shoulders faded.

She gave up trying to keep centimeters between their bodies. Her full breasts flattened against his chest, and this time, he shuddered. Her breasts had featured in a few of his fantasies over the years.

"Are you propositioning me?" Despite his openness, surprise shaded her words.

"Of course."

"Why?" Lisa sounded intrigued.

He laughed. "Simple. You're sexy." He'd wait to tell her how much he wanted to taste her mouth. He shouldn't tell her he wanted to go down on her, lick her pussy and fuck her with his tongue until she came in shuddering release. Nah, he'd spring that on her later.

Her eyes widened fractionally. "I should tell you that yesterday I accepted a dinner date with another man."

"Do you like him?"

"He seems nice."

"You haven't slept with him."

"What kind of question is that?"

"It's the kind of question a man wants answered, especially if he intends to put moves on a special lady."

"You don't mess around, do you?"

"I know what I want."

"But I'm older—"

Irritated at her for not seeing the possibilities, he lowered his head and smothered her protesting words with his lips. He devoured her mouth, not giving her an opportunity to protest. This was war and he intended to win.

Chapter 2

Time for a Fling

The instant his mouth touched hers, her inner fight faded. Her hands curled behind his neck even as she wondered what the heck she was doing locking lips with a guy she used to babysit. Hot guy admittedly, but that was no excuse.

Sweetheart, stop worrying so much. You know Sam. You know his family. You're attracted to him. Give in. You might even enjoy yourself. Have your fling.

Maybe Janice was right. A one-night stand might make her feel alive again. She couldn't talk to her vibrator, and her vibe certainly never indulged in post-coital cuddles.

Our fling turned into something permanent, sweetheart. You promised me you'd try to open your heart to another man.

Lisa sighed. Mindful of her deathbed promise to David, she kept kissing Sam and opened herself to pleasure. She let her mind drift away, leaving whys and why-nots far behind. She made a shy foray with her tongue. Instantly, Sam took over, driving the kiss and fueling need in her. Their tongues stroked together, with each surge echoing in her pussy, making her needy. Desperate for more.

They were both feline shifters. She knew he'd notice her changed scent in the same way she smelled him. One thing was for sure. This kiss felt good. Really good.

Sam pulled back once the music ceased. "Dance with me again."

"Yes."

They didn't speak. Instead, they allowed their bodies to do their talking for them. A quick brush of lips. His hand drifted down to cup her butt. A whisper of his breath against her ear. The sensations built, layer by layer, the early sizzle in her nipples and pussy growing to a burning ache in her clit.

"Are you staying with your sister?" He broke the silence between them three songs later.

"Yes."

"Come home with me."

Lisa frowned against Sam's chest. "I don't know." He was probably staying with his sister, and she didn't feel right about having a one-nighter in a friend's home.

"Jocelyn and Martin have gone to the Gold Coast. I'm house-sitting. Come home with me. Stay the night."

She wanted to say yes, but her mind wouldn't let go of the fact he was younger.

"Please."

If he'd shown arrogance or too much confidence, she would've rejected him immediately. Instead, she heard a trace of pleading, and his uncertainty loosened her restraint. "All right."

Good grief. She couldn't believe she'd agreed to his proposal. When she should have felt fear or maybe shame, elation filled her. A sense of freedom and accomplishment arrived, and another wave of arousal. Her skimpy panties grew damp while her bare breasts seemed heavy and sensitive as they brushed the bodice of her blue halter-neck dress.

Sam took her arm and led her off the dance floor. When someone jostled her, he wrapped a protective arm around her waist. His lime citrus aftershave with its fresh, crisp tones made her want to burrow even nearer. The boy she'd once babysat stood much taller and broader, making her feel fragile in comparison.

They made their way over to Lisa's sister.

"Janice, Lisa is coming home with me."

"I see." No mistaking the laughter in her sister. "Should I leave the back door open for you?"

Lisa scowled and opened her mouth to remonstrate, to say that of course she'd be home.

Sam didn't miss a beat. "Lock the doors. We'll see you tomorrow."

Janice gave her a swift hug. "Have fun."

Self-consciousness suffused her as she nodded. Sticking her nose in the air, Lisa collected her small clutch bag from under the table.

Janice smirked and whispered in her ear, "Enjoy yourself. You deserve someone sexy like Sam."

Sam hustled her out of the marquee, keeping his arm around her shoulders. Saber Mitchell wandered out in front of them, a mystery woman wearing a red dress tucked under his arm. They disappeared around the corner into the darkness.

"Looks like my cousin, Saber, has found his own lady," Sam whispered in her ear, turning her in the opposite direction.

The last of her trepidation faded, and she hoped the mystery woman enjoyed her night as much as she intended to relish hers.

The drive to the house Sam was looking after could have been weird—a chance for her to build a case full of worries and reasons why she should tell him to drop her off at her sister's house. Instead, Sam told her about the horses he was breeding and training for polo. His enthusiasm and love for the horses on his Northern Canterbury farm came through clearly. She also discovered, to her surprise, that he'd done a stint in the army.

Lisa worked at graphic design, and they ended up discussing websites and the property she owned in Cashmere, a suburb at the southern end of Christchurch.

Kismet, according to Sam. They lived and worked in the same province with a short half-hour car journey separating them. And that was on a slow traffic day. Lisa couldn't help but smile at his boyish glee. The fifteen-minute drive to his sister's place took no time at all.

Sam stopped his SUV in front of the house.

Lisa unfastened her belt and reached for the door.

He leaned over to snatch a kiss. Gentle and tender, it twisted her into knots of confusion and lust. *Let's not forget the desire to have his naked body under her hands with him at her mercy.* When he lifted his head, feline shimmered in his eyes. Somehow, she didn't think she'd be the one calling the shots and it didn't worry her in the slightest.

"Wait there. I'll get the door for you."

Lisa froze under the instant memories. David had always opened doors for her, treating her with care, like something precious. Living alone, she'd become used to doing everything for herself. A shiver worked through her, a yearning for a man to look after her.

Sam opened the passenger door and helped her out. An outside light, presumably on a sensor, flicked on, illuminating the footpath leading to the door. A surge of nerves struck as she stepped inside.

"I should offer you a drink."

"I don't want a drink." Lisa shivered as his fingers glided over her bare back. Now that she'd said yes, all she wanted was him.

"Good." Sam's eyes gleamed as he swept her off her feet. He strode along a dim-lit passage with Lisa clutching his shoulders. "There's a light to the right."

Lisa fumbled in the direction he indicated and switched on the light. They were in a room with a double bed. Sam set her on her feet, his gaze intense and searching and dark with desire.

"Can I undress you?"

"Yes." She swallowed, unable to say or do more.

He knelt in front of her to unbuckle her shoes, the warmth of his hands seeping into her feet and darting up her calves. His fingers skirted upward under the hem of her dress. Their gazes met and she drew a bracing breath. When his fingers smoothed across her inner thighs, her stomach muscles quivered. He knew exactly what his touch was doing to her, the knowledge evident in the devilish quirk of his lips.

He ran a finger along the leg of her panties, his callused skin leaving a trail of sensual destruction rioting through her. She had no defenses against his attack. Instead, she vibrated with need, almost purring out loud like the feline she was. She loved the way he stroked and petted her, constantly touching as if he could never get enough. He tugged her panties down her legs and tossed them aside. "Sit on the edge of the bed."

Bemused, she followed his instructions, sitting primly with her legs together.

Sam grinned. "Uh-uh. Not like that." He gently tugged her toward him and parted her legs at the same time. To keep her balance, she fell back on her elbows. "Perfect."

"Ah, maybe we can play doctors and nurses another time." An attack of nerves. She tried to close her legs so he couldn't see her.

"Don't hide."

"You're not the one with your private parts on display."

"I can see I need to work faster to distract you." He brushed a kiss on her inner knee while his busy fingers traced the delicate skin of her inner thighs. "You're beautiful."

"So why can't we both get naked and start fooling around?"

"I don't think I can control myself." He kissed her leg again, moving upward. She swallowed, her stomach bucking with nerves, excitement. "When I get inside you, it's not going to take much for me to explode. I want to make you feel good first."

Oh god. She understood. Right now, she'd detonate at his first touch. Their dancing had come close to foreplay and...

His tongue stroked along her folds and teased her clit. The muscles of her inner thighs quivered, her pulse spiking sharply at the rough lap of his tongue. A hungry whimper escaped her, a tickle of heat pulsing everywhere he licked. Each soft, tormenting stroke sent sensual flames zapping along her veins.

"Sam." Her hips bucked, driving her inflamed flesh against his tongue. She shuddered. "Sam."

He pushed two fingers past her entrance, the intrusion filling an emptiness she hadn't been aware of until now.

Her hands lowered to grip his skull. She tugged his hair, attempting to direct his mouth to where she needed it most. Direct stimulation. Now—to cure the intense ache inside her sex.

"Sam, please make me come now." She yanked his hair to reinforce her words.

"Ouch, woman."

"*Sam.*" This time his name was a plea.

His husky laugh filled the room, the burst of hot air against her tender nub almost more than she could bear. She wriggled and squirmed, attempting to increase the pressure. The wet sound of his fingers stroking in and out of her should have embarrassed her but just drove her urgency higher.

"Now, Lisa." Promise shimmered in his words, making her believe. She sucked in a hoarse breath, and when his mouth closed over her clit and sucked, she released it in a scream. Pleasure ripped through her, darting down her legs and swelling through her upper torso. Her vagina contracted in repeated ripples around his fingers, the spasms going on for long moments. Gradually the explosions quieted and her tense muscles relaxed.

Sam removed his fingers and stood in a fluid move. His hands went to his shirt, and without taking his gaze off her, he started undoing the buttons. "Take off your dress, Lisa.

If it's not off by the time I'm naked, I won't be responsible for damages."

The unvarnished need in his face had her standing on shaky legs. Trembling fingers managed the side zipper of her dress and unfastened the button behind her neck. The fabric slid from her torso and down her hips. Cool air washed over her breasts, making her nipples tighten.

"You're gorgeous." He moved before she'd studied her fill of him, scooping her off her feet and tossing her on the bed instead. He followed her down, the hard contours of his face intent and hungry. His lips settled on hers as he nudged her legs apart.

Sam buried himself in Lisa's wet core with one seamless stroke. She stretched to accommodate him, hot flesh clinging and massaging his shaft. So much better than his imagination. So much better. He wanted to go slow, to make this last for as long as possible. Didn't happen. Luckily, the strain on his features didn't seem to scare her. With each hard stroke, a purr of pleasure escaped. He enjoyed the rumble of sound and smiled. Something to tease her about later.

"Wrap your legs around me, sweetheart."

"Like this?" Not even the endearment that used to be David's threw her off stride.

"Yeah. Perfect." Slipping his hand between their straining bodies, he gave her clit some extra attention. She snatched a deep breath and let out one of her sexy purrs. Seconds later, rhythmic pulses of her channel almost short-circuited his brain. He moaned and thrust into her clinging warmth. Invading. Retreating while Lisa clutched his back, her fingernails digging into his flesh. His breaths came faster, his heart pounding with each rapid stroke. His balls drew up and his cock swelled. A faint tingle started in his nuts and he felt the surge of come as it blasted up his cock and he exploded.

Gasping for breath, Sam slipped from Lisa and drew her into his arms. "Hell, I didn't use a condom." And he couldn't find it in himself to care. Imagining her round with his child gave him a sense of satisfaction.

"I'm taking birth control shots."

Disappointment slammed him first, followed by a sliver of jealousy. It crawled through his gut, taking him by surprise. Man, he was a goner. He drew in a careful breath, fighting the urge to ask why since her husband died some time ago.

As if she sensed his inner turmoil, she added, "You're the first man I've even considered sleeping with since... The shots help my cycle."

Relief filled him at her admission and he started to kiss her again, everywhere he could reach. Her face, her throat, her breasts and taut nipples.

"I want you again," he whispered against her breast. He pictured himself plunging into her from behind, one hand tweaking a nipple and the other delicately playing her clit. And as the tiny quivers started in her pussy, he'd sink his teeth into the marking site, claiming her as his mate. Blood surged into his cock when the vision played through his mind.

"Yes."

Her instant agreement and quick smile gave him confidence. "Can I take you from behind?"

This time silence greeted his question, and when he checked her expression, he found a furrow between her brows. "This is a fling. One night then we go our separate ways."

"I want more." This wasn't the time for pussyfooting around. He refused to let her go without a fight.

"But I'm so much old—"

Sam clapped his hand over her mouth. "You are perfect for me. You're smart and sexy, you know my family and you're a leopard shifter. You're the woman for me. My other half. Tell me you don't feel the heat between us, the pull to take things further."

She turned away but not before he caught her gnawing on her bottom lip. He grasped her arm when she attempted to roll off the bed.

"Lisa, give us a chance. Say you'll go out with me. Tell the other man you're taken. Come and stay with me during the weekends. Let me woo you. Let me prove to you how good things could be between us."

The desperation in his tone stilled Lisa, made her pause. Sam was right. They were good together, but a future? She shook her head as common sense warred with her gut instinct.

He's a good man, sweetheart. He cares for you, will cherish and love you. Give him a chance.

David *would* choose this moment to yammer in her mind, when she needed one-hundred-percent focus. And going to bat for his replacement—what sort of haunting was this?

"Lisa?"

She went with David's advice plus her gut, sliding back onto the bed, her lips meeting Sam's. When they parted from their lip-lock, he lifted her over him and she sank onto his cock. She rocked up and down, savoring the friction, the hot pleasure that fluttered through her with each slide.

"Touch your nipples. Pull on them," Sam instructed.

34

She followed his order, tugged at her nipples as she ground against him.

"Can't hang on," he muttered, and he flipped her over, pumping his cock into her in fevered strokes. Lisa clung to him for the ride, shattering a few seconds before he came too.

It was difficult to miss the satisfaction in him. His face and eyes glowed with it, yet he refrained from smartass comments. Instead, he sighed with contentment, regarding her with a lazy grin.

"What?"

"There's so much I want to do with your sexy body. I don't know where to start."

Lisa wriggled and tightened her inner muscles in order to tease him. He was still partially erect, the drag of his flesh over her clit firing a ball of heat at her.

"Don't start something you don't want to finish," he warned.

She pulled free and pushed him flat on the mattress. "I want to explore you."

Grinning, he raised his hands and placed them under his head. "Have at it, sweetheart. Do your worst."

"Leave your hands right where they are." Somehow David's approval and the familiar endearment, said in

Sam's sexy drawl, made their escapade right and settled her immediate objections, allowed her to relax into teasing.

"Yes, ma'am."

Lisa snorted. Sam might behave like a lazy housecat right now, but she recognized the disguise. He was a sleek jungle beast in his prime. Velvet tension bloomed in her, tugging at her breasts and her restraint. She couldn't wait to see him in his feline form, to run with him and experience the wind rushing over her fur. Once he shifted, he'd be bigger than her. She stared at his bulging pectorals, his ridged abs and let her attention wander to his flat stomach.

"Are you gonna touch me anytime soon?"

"Shush," she chided. "I'm trying to decide where to touch first." Her eyes strayed lower to his cock and her tongue darted out to moisten her lips. His shaft pulsed and thickened while she watched. Her gaze darted up to meet his. "Don't even think it. This is my turn."

Sam smirked. "I bet you take forever to open your presents."

A subtle warning. If she didn't hurry, he'd take over again. She leaned nearer and nibbled one pectoral muscle. He tasted salty—a little spicy. And he was all hers to explore. A kiss. A leisurely flick of tongue across a nipple. Her mouth headed south, following in the wake of her busy fingers. Already, his erection dug into her hip.

"I can think of a place that needs attention."

Lisa smiled against his abdomen, tracing her lips down the delicate skin where his torso and leg met. "Where would that be? Here?" She lightly bit his upper thigh, silently laughing at his huff of complaint. "Here?" She moved to his inner thigh. "Or here?" Finally, she closed her mouth around the tip of his cock.

"Perfect choice."

Lisa gave up her teasing and settled in to give him pleasure. Each sound, each shudder she pulled from him gave her enjoyment in return. Soon he was rocking into her mouth, his breathing unsteady as she made greedy, slurping sounds and sucked him off. His hands came down to grip her skull, the tug of his fingers in her hair bringing an echo of sensation in her. Without warning, he pulled from her touch and tossed her on her back.

"I don't want to come alone," he said, rubbing her swollen clit with a firm motion. He slid into her, sank deep and pinched her nub. Lisa came so hard she saw stars. Sam followed her into orgasm, holding her for long moments afterward.

Her loud yawn brought a chuckle. "Have I tired you out, sweetheart?"

"A little." She'd experience a few aches and pains tomorrow in limbs unused to vigorous lovemaking. Not that she cared.

He tugged back the covers and helped her underneath, drawing her into his arms. "We have a future, Lisa. Let me prove it."

"All right," she whispered. "We can see how things work out."

"We're good together. You'll see." Sam kissed her one last time, and she fell asleep with a smile on her face.

Chapter 3

Investigation and Date

Lisa wanted to stay in Middlemarch, to cling to the memories of a spectacular weekend. She smiled as the familiar piles of schist rock, the valley and range of mountains surrounding the country town disappeared in her rear-vision mirror. Sam had already left, needed back at his farm because one of his employees had fallen and couldn't work.

I told you this weekend would refresh you.

Lisa sniffed in a very feline way. David might not have possessed feline genes but his constant yammering in her head smacked of freaky power. She couldn't quite decide if the conversations were the product of her conscience or if David truly haunted her. She'd considered seeking a second opinion from her sister or a doctor then quashed the idea. As far as she knew, she was sane and found comfort in David's presence.

No one else needed to know.

Well?

A chuckle escaped her. "I enjoyed myself. I hope you kept your eyes shut."

Not telling.

"Humph."

What are you going to do about your date?

"I think I'll go and play it by ear. If he asks me out again, I'll say no. He's an adult. I'm sure it will be fine. Besides, the Oberon is a classy restaurant. I doubt he'd create a scene."

You'll be careful?

"Janice told you before we decided to get married that careful and cautious were my middle names."

Ah, but she doesn't know you like I do. You have a wild streak, my love.

Lisa smiled, knowing his words or her thought—whichever—bore more than a smidgeon of truth. She did possess a wild streak that led her into flings, for a start.

Sam. A younger man. Who would've thought?

There was an age gap with us.

"But it's different with a man."

Why?

Lisa pulled up at a stop sign, waited until the traffic cleared and drove onto the main road leading to Christchurch.

You should look it up on the internet.

A snort erupted at the advice. "Now I know it's my own mind rather than a haunting. You disliked computers."

But I know Google. Everyone knows about search engines. Very useful things when you want information.

"Maybe I will," she said and reached forward to switch on some music. "Hush now and let me concentrate. It looks as if everyone has decided to hit the road at the same time as me."

Tyler wore a disguise. He'd donned a wig of dark cinnamon brown, making his hair longer and curlier than his usual style. He'd also applied chin scruff and made his cheeks appear rounder. His jeans, T-shirt and scuffed brown leather jacket cried pure biker, and now he straddled his bike and rode toward Lisa's home in Cashmere.

Eagerness pulsed through his body, an echo of the vibrations from his black Harley.

James's enthusiasm had rubbed off on him, and he couldn't wait to get his first in-person glance of Lisa Jordan. He turned onto her road at half-past six, and prayed he'd catch her before she left for her date. Not that this trip would be wasted. He'd wanted to scout her house and grounds, check out the neighbors and security in the area.

He rode at the speed limit, taking in the houses and watching the numbers. Ten. Fourteen. Ah, there. Number twenty, Beechwood Drive. Large house for one person. An older wooden dwelling with an enormous private section. A home that would be sought after because of its historical significance. Mature trees in the garden. He caught a flash of a charcoal-gray car but not enough to discern the make and model. Excellent. This property appeared low security and offered myriad places to hide while he watched.

He parked opposite and pulled out his phone. While he pretended to take a call, he watched her driveway, the neighbors' driveways and the other activity in the quiet street.

An elderly lady opened the door of the two-story brick home next to number twenty and led out a shaggy Jack Russell dog. Petite with a lived-in face and bird-sharp eyes, she scanned him as she and her mutt ambled past him. He ignored her and spoke to his nonexistent caller until she turned onto Fergus Crescent, the road leading to the park.

A car slowed and pulled into the house opposite. A man in a suit climbed out of a late-model car and juggled his briefcase and keys while speaking on the phone pressed to his ear. He never even glanced at Tyler.

Still, it wouldn't do to dally too long because the elderly woman appeared the nosy type. If the beautiful Lisa didn't appear in the next five minutes, he'd drive down the road and wait there for the length of another pretend phone call.

But as he put his phone away, the gray sedan—a late-model Toyota—drove down the driveway toward him and he got his first sighting of Lisa Jordan.

She wore dark glasses and had restrained her black hair at the back of her neck. That was all he saw, but it was enough to confirm her identity.

Tyler balanced his Harley, waiting for her to pull out before he followed. Not one curtain twitched at his departure. No neighborhood watch. Good for their purposes. Skulking around in preparation for the game filled him with joyous anticipation. *Too much fun.*

As he followed Lisa down Beechwood Drive, he noted a few yards with kids' toys, but most were older houses, set back from the road with mature trees and places to remain concealed if necessary. The familiar buzz of excitement ratcheted up a notch. His latest book had drained him physically and mentally, and this new game might prove just the thing to refill his creative well.

The restaurant, Christchurch

Lisa found a parking space and drew in a quick breath to steady her nerves. Silly really. James seemed a nice man, and they'd conversed easily with graphic design and advertising in common.

But now that she'd met Sam again, and promised to give their fledgling relationship a try, she felt weird meeting James for dinner.

Originally, she'd planned to tell him at the end of the night, but no. That didn't feel right. She'd confess as soon as she saw him, give him the option of cutting the night short. With that thought in mind, she exited her car, locked it and hurried to the restaurant entrance.

"Lisa, you're here. Right on time." James wore a black suit with a white shirt and a blue-and-gold striped tie. He rose from his seat at the bar and beamed at her, his smile white and his hazel eyes friendly. "They've been busy, and our table isn't quite ready. Would you like a drink first?"

"That would be lovely." She wore one of her vintage dresses in a blue-and-white floral with a navy-blue bolero and was glad she'd gone to the trouble since this restaurant—one she hadn't been to before—seemed on the formal side.

"Did you have an enjoyable weekend?" James stood aside for her to slip into a chair in a window alcove. He took the seat opposite and signaled for service. "What would you like?"

"A glass of Sauvignon Blanc would be perfect. Yes, I always enjoy getting home to Middlemarch."

She and Sam had managed a quick run with his cousins, the Mitchells. She'd enjoyed the rare treat, running through the countryside without worrying about witnesses, running with other shifters in feline form. Not that she could talk about the treat with James. His scent indicated he was one-hundred-percent human.

"What about you?" She smiled at him once he'd ordered wine for her and a second glass for him. "Did you enjoy your weekend?"

"I'm afraid I had to spend the weekend working on a rush job for a client," James said. "At least we managed to get the campaign completed and we have a happy client. And my reward is dinner with a beautiful woman."

"Thank you." Lisa smiled as he meant her to, yet something in his cheerful behavior ruffled her inner feline. It was almost as if he was trying too hard. No. No, she was being too hard on him, mentally comparing him to Sam with his casual ease. "Actually, there is something I need to tell you." She forced herself to look him in the eye and thought she caught a flicker of something. Maybe irritation? But it faded almost as quickly as it appeared.

He smiled. "Go ahead."

Pleasant affability. That was all that she saw when she returned the polite smile. No, her nerves were making her imagine things. A guilty conscience.

"I met an old friend in Middlemarch. We hit it off, and I've agreed to see him again." She paused to test his reaction and let the rest of her words pour from her. "I feel bad. I hate to lead you on. I'll go." She made to stand, but James laid his hand on her forearm.

"Stay," he said. "It's refreshing to find a woman of integrity. Stay and have dinner with me. We can be friends, can't we?"

Lisa felt her shoulders sag, and she dropped onto her chair again. "I...are you sure you still want to have dinner with me?"

"I'm sure. Who wouldn't want to have dinner with a beautiful woman? Tell me what you're working on at present with your graphic business. It's not a secret?"

Lisa relaxed at his casual conversation. "My current job is designing graphics for a cupcake bakery. It's a fun project, but I've put on weight. They keep giving me cupcakes to sample."

"You're stunning," he said, an appreciative glow lighting his features. "I bet cupcakes are easier to work into a campaign than the tractors and diggers I have at present."

A waitress arrived with their drinks and once she bustled away, Lisa took a sip, savoring the hints of stone fruit and passionfruit. Delicious.

"Are you attending the Design Awards dinner next week?" he asked.

"Yes, one of my designs is up for an award. It's the first time I've ever received a nomination." A burst of pride filled her, since she knew she did good work, and peer recognition helped her grow her business.

"Congratulations. I'll see you there. Are you bringing anyone with you?"

Lisa hesitated. This thing with Sam seemed so new, and she wasn't ready to go public with the relationship yet. At least, not here in the city. "Not so far."

James took a sip of his wine. "I don't have a date either. Would it be against the friendship rules to ask you to sit with me?"

"No, of course not. I'd love the company, although I warn you, nerves might get the better of me."

He patted her hand. "Good, that's settled. I'll meet you there, and we'll sit together. Not a date, but two friends sharing another meal."

"Thank you. That sounds lovely."

"Sir, your table is ready now. Would you like to go through?"

James looked askance at her, and she nodded. No drama or hurt feelings. He was nice.

Two minutes later, James seated her at a table in another bay window alcove. The windows looked out over a local park and formal gardens that were ablaze with flowers. Lisa couldn't name the flower varieties, but the gardens drew the eye with the vibrant colors, visible under strategically placed spotlights. Even though she lacked a green thumb, she could appreciate nature and beauty when she witnessed it.

The waitress offered Lisa a menu and the next few minutes they discussed the various dishes.

"Have you decided?" James asked.

"I'll have the sirloin steak please," Lisa said.

"Oh? You surprise me."

"Why? Because it's not fashionable to eat red meat?"

"Yes."

"I don't like to follow trends," Lisa said. All she could say since she'd never confess her feline tendencies to James. She kept coming back to the word "nice" because it fit. Everything about him slotted into an average pigeonhole, which was overly critical on her part. Or maybe Sam's appearance in her life made him seem ordinary. Her stomach gave a little swoop of excitement. Sam had given her his phone number and perhaps she'd call him once she returned home.

"Do you visit your family often? Or do you have family here in Christchurch?"

"My sister and her family live in Middlemarch. I have friends and cousins there, but I don't get to visit a lot."

"How did you end up in Christchurch?"

Small chitchat. She'd manage to get through this dinner after all. "I met my husband while working up in Auckland. I had a trainee position at one of the big advertising agencies there, and he was a client. We hit it off and married six months later. David, my husband, came from Christchurch, so it seemed better for me to relocate. I've grown to enjoy it here."

"Despite the spates of earthquakes."

"In spite of the earthquakes. I was lucky since my house didn't suffer any damage. How about you?"

"I live on the outskirts of Christchurch and we got through the shakes remarkably unscathed. I lost friends though."

Silence fell as Lisa thought of the two girlfriends, lost due to the second big quake.

"A bad time," James murmured. "Let's agree to change the subject. What made you decide to go into business on your own?"

"I'd been talking about it for a while. My husband encouraged me to start on my own, and it turned into a blessing. After David became sick, I worked from home while spending time with him."

"You're very young to have lost a husband." He patted her hand, and she took comfort from the contact. "It must have been difficult."

Lisa glanced down at her lap, finding herself flung back into the dark days of David's death. She still missed him, which was probably why he haunted her days and spoke to her. It was her way of coping. "This isn't a very cheerful topic either. Do you enjoy sports? I am an avid rugby fan and the best armchair referee I know. I cheer for the Canterbury Crusaders."

"I enjoy cricket and play in a summer league and also enjoy the odd round of golf."

"Oh, dear," Lisa said with mock sorrow. "I don't think we can be friends after all."

James stared at her for an instant, then barked out a laugh that had several of their neighboring diners staring at them.

A giggle erupted from Lisa and they grinned at each other. "What about music? Television shows? You go first."

"I enjoy jazz."

Lisa wrinkled her nose and his grin widened. "I'm rock and roll all the way. I will listen to pop and enjoy some of it, but I prefer rock. Books?"

"Thrillers," he said solemnly.

Lisa clapped a hand to her breast. "Oh, no!"

"You?"

"Romances and mysteries." She watched him closely, and he scarcely blinked at her confession. A nice guy, she thought again, but he didn't possess the alpha tendencies that attracted her to Sam. Then, there was the feline thing. Her run with Sam had left her dizzy with pleasure, especially since they'd stolen a little time alone to smooch. "Television?"

"True crime shows."

"That does it," Lisa said. "We absolutely cannot be friends." Her phone rang and she plucked it from her handbag and scanned the screen. "I'm so sorry, but I have to get this. It's a last-minute change to an ad campaign."

"You go ahead. I'll take the opportunity to use the restroom."

"Thank you." Lisa answered the call. "Malcolm, it's good to hear from you. Have you and your board made a decision on the final details?"

James stood and wove through the tables of diners, his route taking him past Tyler as he headed for the restroom. The scent of cooking steaks came from the direction of the kitchen and he paused to allow a waitress past. She carried a starter platter of canapes plus a pepper grinder as long as her arm. Another waitress exited the kitchen, and he gestured her to continue when she hesitated with her load of meals. With his way clear, he strode down a corridor to the men's washroom. After a quick check of the stalls, he checked his appearance while he waited for his twin.

Tyler entered a few minutes later. "Problem?"

"Yeah. She told me she met someone over the weekend. I like her, Tyler. She's upfront and honest."

His twin frowned at him. "What are you trying to tell me? What do you want to do?"

"I managed to keep my temper. I've been working on that."

"Good. That's good." Tyler nodded, his blue eyes—thanks to contacts—glowing with approval.

James felt the ball of tension in his gut dissolve. He *had* done well. He'd taken previous lessons to heart and learned from mistakes made during their first games in Auckland. "I might not be the guy she sleeps with, but we can still play the game. We can amend the rules. I was thinking we could have a score sheet and receive points for tasks. And if one of us happens to be the friend she turns to, so much the better."

"You want to punish her."

James shrugged, for once uncertain, but taking pains to hide it from his brother. "Goes without saying, but I want her to have a chance to change her mind about me too. She is smart and clever and her integrity places her above most women of my acquaintance. You'll see when you meet her."

"You don't need to sell me on this game." Tyler's voice held the gritty affection that always soothed James. It worked this time too, dispersing the last of his angst and the sense of a failed task. "I'm in. I might leave the restaurant now and see if I can get into her house. I'll try to discover the name of the man she's seeing. Okay?"

James nodded. "I'll try to spin out the dinner to give you plenty of time."

"Ten points to your scoreboard if you can keep her out after ten."

"I work well with a challenge."

"I know." Tyler sounded smug. "Ten points to me if I can discover the name of her man."

"Done," James said and he gave his twin a quick, affectionate hug. "It's good to have you home again. I've missed you. Calls and email from the US aren't the same as seeing you in person."

Chapter 4

Intruder Trouble

It was after eleven when Lisa arrived home from her date. She pushed the remote for her garage door and drove straight into the attached garage. A yawn erupted as she grabbed her handbag and climbed from her car, tired but buzzed. Her phone call *had* held bad news—for her campaign, at least. The client wanted something completely different. She'd been ready to call off dinner and head home, but James had persuaded her to discuss the campaign and the client's needs. He'd offered to brainstorm. *Nice man.*

Now, she had a kickass idea. Two, actually, and she itched to get started.

She pushed the remote to shut the garage and opened the connecting door, freezing one step into her house.

A scent. A foreign one had her dragging air over her receptors. Someone had...

A tight band around her chest reminded her to breathe. Her held breath whooshed out, another in, as she rapidly scanned her passage, feline sight piercing the shadows. The muscles in her legs coiled, ready to spring into motion.

A minute passed. Two.

Nothing happened.

Lisa forced her locked knees to move in jerky steps down the passage toward her kitchen. At the doorway, she halted, listening. The hum of the fridge. The drip of her tap. *Cowboy plumber.*

Not a sound out of place.

Lisa reached around to flick on the lights, the illumination spilling from the kitchen into the passage. She paused to allow her eyes to become used to the light. The plumber had visited yesterday to fix a leaking pipe and would need to return. She hadn't come in this way earlier, so she hadn't noticed anything unusual. She tiptoed in the direction of the scent and frowned when the trail didn't fade. Instead, it intensified, and she blinked in sync with her pulse rate.

The citrus scent—not unpleasant but wrong—wafted on the air.

Her fingers tightened on the strap of her handbag, an ache springing to life at her temples, a sense of shock. Disbelief.

A stranger had stood in her kitchen.

After checking behind her, she placed her bag on the counter and pulled out her phone, her gaze sweeping all four corners of her designer kitchen.

Be careful, Lisa. David's deep tones echoed in her mind. *They might still be in the house.*

Her ring tone blasted through the silence without warning. She jumped, letting out a feminine *eep* before her mind told her the source of the noise. "H-hello?"

"Sweetheart? Are you all right?" Sam's husky tones had her tension receding.

"I've just arrived home from my date."

"I thought you were telling him to get lost."

She smiled wryly. *Hello, Mr. Alpha.* "I told him I'd met someone else as soon as we sat down for a pre-dinner drink at the bar. He said he was sorry to hear that, but he'd enjoy being friends and persuaded me to stay for dinner. I thought it might be uncomfortable, but he's a nice guy."

"So why do you sound flustered?"

"I think someone has been in my house while I've been away. There is a strange scent. The plumber came yesterday, but I didn't notice anything earlier."

"Ring the cops."

"And tell them what? My feline can smell a scent that shouldn't be here? I haven't had a chance to check it out yet. Maybe it's a burglary." One of the reasons she'd left Middlemarch. She didn't do bossy males. While David had been strong and masculine, he'd always listened to her opinion and not treated her like a helpless ninny.

"Stay on the phone while you check."

Lisa took the phone from her ear and pulled a face at it before replying. "Sam, I will. I'll describe everything I can see and smell."

"Be careful." The gruff words held worry and concern.

"I'm in the kitchen. Nothing missing that I can see. My laptop is still where I left it earlier. Following the scent trail now." She flipped light switches as she crept through the various rooms—the dining room, the lounge—searching the corners and behind furniture. While she didn't say it out loud, having Sam on the other end of the phone pushed away her initial fears. "The scent is stronger in some places, but I can't see anything missing."

"Okay." Sam sounded more relaxed now. "Do you want me to drive to your place?"

"It's late. Just wait while I check upstairs in the bedrooms." Lisa paused to switch on the light at the base of the broad wooden staircase. Made from native kauri, it was a real showpiece. The first and the last two stairs creaked. She and David had always joked their kids would have to climb out the window to creep from the house. Unfortunately, they'd never had children to test the theory. She scented the air, her unease deepening again at finding the trail without difficulty. "He or she went upstairs. They must have known I'd gone out because the stairs creak."

"Keep talking to me."

"How was your day? Is your guy recovering from his fall?"

"He broke his leg," Sam said in disgust. "I need more shifters working for me."

"You don't mean that. The scent of predator must frighten the horses." Lisa climbed the staircase. *Creak. Creak. Creak.* The sound that had always made her smile now failed to amuse her. If someone loitered up there waiting for her, they'd know she'd arrived home. They would've heard her car and the garage door. Nerves tap-danced in the pit of her stomach, the sense of trespass making her twitchy. Her feline twisted beneath her skin, agitated and echoing her unease.

Sam heaved out a hard sigh. "No, I don't mean that. Keith is a good worker. He's been with me since I started breeding horses for polo and showjumping, and him being unable to work means I need to take up the slack."

"Can he do something else for you? A task that doesn't need two legs."

"I'll have to find him a job to do because he's driving me crazy. He's snapping at my other employees. Are you at the top of the stairs yet?"

"Can you hear my knees shaking?"

"I can be there in half an hour."

"No. You're tired and it's late. I have a secret advantage."

"Unless the intruder has a gun."

"Stop trying to scare me. Guns are mostly illegal in New Zealand."

"Try telling that to the criminal element," Sam countered. "Hell, I shouldn't have said that. It's frustrating being here when you need me."

A flash of irritation replaced the anxiety that had taken hold of her. "I am older than you. I know how to look after myself. I've been doing it since before David died."

"I know. You're right. It's my feline side. He wants to protect you now that we've found you."

"Well, haul your feline up by the scruff of the neck. Going to check the bedrooms now. Spare ones first." She turned on lights, checked wardrobes, the family bathroom, the restroom, the storage cupboards in the hall, her irritation at Sam's bossy tendencies shoving aside her trepidation. "Nothing. I can't see anything missing."

"Can you still smell the intruder's scent?"

"Yes, he or she had a good wander around my house. I'm checking my bedroom and en suite now." The scent smelled stronger here, as if the intruder held high emotions. Male, she decided. "I think the intruder is male. It's a citrus aftershave I can smell." She peered into her en suite, her wardrobe—not that he'd fit in there, given the surplus of clothes—and under the bed. A cool breeze had her turning toward the dual-aspect windows. One of the windows facing the rear gardens stood open. "One of the windows is open." She sniffed and the last of the tension in her shoulders lifted. "He went out the window. I hate the idea of someone going through my things."

"Do you have anything to make them suspect you're a shifter?"

"No, nothing like that."

"But you said your husband knew."

"He did. I loved him." Silence fell—uncomfortable and tense. "Sorry," she said. "This has made me a little tense."

"I'm sorry too," Sam said. "Put your phone on speaker and talk to me while you get ready for bed. Wish I was there."

His fervent tone raised a giddy happiness—joy a woman her age had no right to feel. "I have an awards dinner next week. Would you come with me?" An impulse, but it felt right, despite what she'd told James earlier.

"Yes," he said without hesitation and she found herself smiling. "Are you up for an award?"

"I am. I doubt whether I'll win but it's excellent publicity for my business."

"Hell, there's someone at the door. It'd better not be Keith. I'll break his other leg for him."

Lisa laughed. "Give the man a break." She realized what she'd said and chortled. "Sorry about the pun. Answer the door."

"I'll ring you back."

"You don't have to."

"I want to. Don't break down my door. I'm coming," he hollered. "Talk to you soon, sweetheart."

Lisa glanced at her dresser, her hairbrush and comb and a bottle of perfume, a pearl necklace David had given her and the matching pair of earrings on the surface. She prowled across the thick woolen rug David had purchased in Turkey and studied the mostly smooth covers of her king-size bed. Her sense of violation increased on spotting the wrinkles on the bottom corner.

A backside imprint. The intruder had rested his butt there.

His scent coated everything in her bedroom.

Lisa spun to survey her open wardrobe and clothing hung from several partially open drawers Maybe she'd sleep in the downstairs bedroom, the one David had used during the last weeks of his life and she'd turned into an office to meet with clients. And maybe she'd reconsider a security alarm. The huge quote she'd received... Well, she'd wanted to plow her money into advertising her business.

She did another round of her house, checking each window and door to ensure it was secure. Someone had invaded her sanctuary.

Her phone rang and she jumped at the blast of noise. With a hammering heart, she plucked it from her pocket and checked the incoming number. "You didn't have to ring me back."

"I wanted to. Two of my army buddies have shown up. They're having a few weeks off while they decide where to set up their new business. You'll never guess what type of business."

"Growing pickles," she said promptly and grinned at the silence.

"I love a woman with a sense of humor."

"Good to know."

"They're setting up a security business. They're both shifters. Henry is a wolf and Gerard is feline. Maybe they could scope out your place."

"Tomorrow," she said firmly. "I intend to shift to feline and curl up on the couch in the office."

"Are you sure—"

"Positive, Sam. I'll check everything more thoroughly tomorrow in the daylight, but I can't see anything missing. Probably one of the neighborhood kids who broke in on a dare. David and I caught several teenagers trying to break in a few years ago."

"Promise you'll ring if you need me."

"I promise." She hung up with a smile, but then she caught a trace of the scent again and cold fingers drifted down her spine. Maybe she'd check the house again before she attempted to sleep.

It was a horrid sensation—not feeling secure in her own home, and Lisa didn't sleep well. She woke several times, lifting her furred head to catalog the varied creaks and shifting noises her house made, searching for anything out of place. Finally, at dawn, she climbed off the couch in her office and padded to the middle of the room to stretch. With regret, she shifted to human form and pulled on her silky navy-blue robe. Maybe a run would help sweep the cobwebs from her brain.

Five minutes later, with phone, cash and keys in her pockets, she left her house in exercise gear. She fell into the comforting rhythm of jogging, her breathing slow and easy as she ran through the early morning. Unseen birds chortled and cheeped in joyous song, far perkier than her.

As she attacked a hill, her mind went to her intruder. Why? That was the big question. Why would someone break into her home and not take anything? Heck, maybe they had, and she hadn't noticed yet. On the flat, she extended her stride, waving to old Mr. Jenkins who never slept much either. She often saw him collecting his newspaper. She ran along a narrow path, through the park, the grassy surface shining with morning dew. As usual, the exercise calmed her, energized her and appeased the restlessness of her feline.

David had suggested she start the daily routine because he'd worried about her feline side. A sudden tightness gripped her chest. David had made sure they'd had a few days every month in a place where she could shift and embrace her feline nature.

Sweetheart, don't be sad. Our time together was perfect. We had fun and we loved each other, complemented each other. You've met Sam now, and I couldn't be happier. He's a good man and you will work well together.

Lisa snorted. "He's already tried to boss me around."

He was worried and frustrated because he couldn't be with you. Cut him some slack.

"Maybe."

She passed another runner and he gave her an odd look. *Now look what you've done. He thinks I'm ready for the funny farm.*

You talk to me all the time. Maybe you are ready to check in.

"Funny man."

I try.

She ran around the park three times, savoring the feel of the grass beneath her feet and the slight give of the softer ground. Her muscles had warmed and the faint sheen of perspiration coated her limbs. A glance at her watch told her she should head back. She'd grab a coffee on the way and plunge into her workday. She'd ring for security quotes too.

Lisa jogged to the cafe, not far from her house, and ordered a latte. She sat outside at one of the round silver tables and watched the rest of her neighborhood start their morning. Her phone rang.

"Sam, how are you?"

"You're not at home."

Oops, Mr. Alpha again—not the charming Sam of the night of the singles dance. "No, I had trouble sleeping, so I started my morning run earlier than normal. I stopped for a caffeine fix. Wait, how do you know I'm not at home?"

"Because I'm parked in your driveway." He dragged in an audible breath, as if struggling for control. "Sorry. I shouldn't have snapped. I was worried when you weren't here."

"I'll be home in about ten minutes, if you can wait."

"I can wait." His voice dropped to low and husky and held none of his earlier irritation. Her stomach did a little flip-flop. It was nice having someone worry about her.

When Lisa jogged up her drive, she found Sam chatting with two big males. They all stood to attention at her arrival.

"Lisa." The warmth in Sam's voice and his open happiness on seeing her canceled the faint trepidation she'd harbored about meeting him again. "This is my friend, Henry." He pointed to the beefy man on his right. Long dark blond hair framed a face of hard angles. Deep chocolate-brown eyes sliced and diced before he offered a faint smile and a curt nod. Wolf, she thought.

"And this is Gerard."

Gerard, although as big as Henry, didn't have the same bulk. He kept his black hair shorter and on the shaggy side. An attractive male, one who used flirtation to good effect.

He grinned at her, a feline smirk. "Sam, my man, you never said she was so pretty."

Sam rolled his eyes. "Why would I tell you? You'll try to steal her away from me."

Gerard took her hand and lightly squeezed, his pale green eyes full of laughter as he winked at her. "Yes."

"I'm older than all of you," Lisa said in a stern teacher voice.

Sam growled. He actually growled and her eyes widened in shock. "I thought we'd sorted that out while we were in Middlemarch. Say something like that again, and I *will* put you over my knee and spank you."

A flush of heat converged in her cheeks and when she risked a glance at Gerard and Henry, she found them both grinning.

"You shouldn't ignore his warning," Henry said in a gruff voice. "He never makes idle threats."

Lisa tamped down her discomfort and forced herself to look at Gerard. "Is that true?"

"Yes."

Finally, she glanced at Sam. "Sorry, I'll try not to slip again." He was right to remind her. She'd turned down James in favor of Sam, since she enjoyed the weekend and their time together immensely. After her initial shock, the age difference hadn't seemed to matter. Doubts only surfaced once they parted.

"Sam said you had an intruder. Did you check outside and around the window he exited?" Henry asked.

"No, I hadn't thought of it. I intended to recheck the interior in case I missed something last night. Come inside, and I'll make breakfast for us all."

"Do you have meat?" Gerard asked.

"Yes, I have meat. I'm a feline shifter." Lisa unlocked the door and led them inside. "I thought you were short-staffed."

"Henry and Gerard helped me with the morning chores. And one of Keith's friends showed up. He's willing to help until Keith is more mobile."

"Can we check out the scent trail?" Henry asked.

"Sure. Go ahead while I sort out breakfast."

Sam gestured his friends to leave and took her into his arms. "Sorry I've been snappish and bossy. I *was* worried."

"It's a feline thing. You all turn bossy."

Sam pulled back with a frown clouding his features. "Is that why you married a human?"

"I married David because I loved him. Nothing to do with race or species. But you should know I've grown independent."

"It's part of what I like about you. But you should know, I'll probably become bossy again and attempt to order you around."

"I might obey you." She patted his cheek, secretly enjoying the roughness of his cheek. "And I might not. It will depend on the circumstances. You'd better let me start breakfast. My tummy feels as if it's turning inside out."

"Can't have your beautiful curves melting away." His hand skimmed her breasts, the lightness of his touch making her yearn for a greater pressure. She bit back the moan building in her throat and wrapped her arms around his broad shoulders, offering her mouth for a kiss.

"I missed you," he whispered, seconds before he took her mouth.

She expected fast, hard, passionate. She received soft, thorough and toe-curling sexy. *Wow. Just wow.* She leaned her weight against his chest and sank into the pleasure of Sam's touch. Her fingers burrowed through his black hair, holding him as he held her close.

She didn't know what it was about Sam, but he'd cemented himself into her life so quickly. She'd missed him too and wished they could spend the rest of the day together. For the first time ever, the temptation to toss aside work commitments fluttered to the surface.

His tongue stroked her bottom lip. Sharp teeth played with it and desire spiked like a lightning strike.

"Sam," she whispered.

"Hey, we're never gonna get food if you don't quit mauling Lisa." Henry's gritted voice disturbed their kiss, but Sam maintained contact with her. "She needs better locks on the windows. Old windows though. Might be costly. You could always put up bars."

"And feel as if I'm living in a jail? No thank you." Lisa pulled free and mourned the loss of contact. He made her feel safe. Happy.

Sam placed his hands on her shoulders and kissed her brow. "We will pick this up where we left off later tonight. You could visit me at the farm and bring work with you, if you need to, but I thought you might enjoy a run. We can run after dark."

"It's a date. I'm designing an ad for a cupcake company, and they've decided on a new website as well, but I can do what I need to before I head to your place."

Unable to resist, Sam gave her another quick kiss and wandered off to speak with his two friends.

"Learn anything?" he asked on finding them in the lounge.

"The bastard spent a while exploring the house. His citrus scent is everywhere," Henry said. "We're going to check outside."

"I'll come with you," Sam said.

Once outside, they wandered the garden.

"Big-ass garden," Gerard said. "Lots of hiding places."

Sam frowned at the mature trees, the hidden spots that weren't visible from the house but would benefit someone wanting to act the Peeping Tom. "We need to find his trail, discover how he arrived or left without detection."

Without further discussion, they spread out to search for the trail.

"I've got it," Henry called.

Unease sat firmly on Sam's shoulders as he followed his friend. Lisa hadn't imagined a thing, and they needed to discover why someone had decided to enter her property, why someone wanted to taunt her. His woman.

Henry grunted. "Bastard took a piss here. Marked his spot."

"A shifter?"

"I can't tell," Gerard said. "Can you?"

Sam moved closer and inhaled, dragging the different complexities of the scent deep into his lungs. "He makes free with the aftershave. It's covered most of his natural scent. Just a hint of musk but not enough to identify him."

"Same," Gerard said. "Henry?"

Of the three, Henry had the best sense of smell. He circled the big totara tree trunk with its many sturdy branches and small evergreen leaves. "I think he waited and watched from here, but I don't get much of his scent either."

"What do we do?" Gerard asked, looking at Sam.

"Not much we can do," Henry said before Sam could reply. "I'd recommend locks on the windows and installing an alarm. You don't have anything you can take to the cops."

"Yeah, that's what I thought."

Lisa came around the corner of the house. "Breakfast is ready. Just gonna grab the newspaper from the box."

"I'll get it," Sam said.

"I have legs."

Sam studied her legs and grinned, then he realized his two mates were ogling her long limbs as well. He elbowed them both. "Mine," he growled.

Henry snorted.

Gerard nudged him back. "Not marked."

"Stop winding him up. He might kick us out of his place," Henry said.

Lisa strode away to collect her paper, and he and his friends wandered to the kitchen.

"Take a seat," Lisa said on entering with the paper. "Sam, would you get the coffee?"

Sam paused at the order in her tone. He decided he liked the crisp demands she fired at him since they made him feel like part of a couple. He grabbed the coffeepot and filled up the four blue mugs that sat on the table.

"There is another ready to go. Can you hit the switch when you replace the coffeepot please?" Lisa pulled a platter of meat from the warming drawer of her oven and placed it on the table. "Anyone want part of the paper?"

"Sports," Gerard said.

"Business section, please," Henry answered.

"Dig in," Lisa said after she placed a dish of scrambled eggs and another of grilled tomatoes on the table. The toast won't be long." The toaster popped up seconds after she uttered the words, and she handed it over and popped down four more slices.

"Smells great," Sam said. "Thanks for making us breakfast."

"No problem. It's nice to have someone to cook for." She helped herself to bacon, sausage and eggs.

Sam couldn't help staring. He'd almost told his sister he couldn't housesit because of farm commitments. Then, he wouldn't have met Lisa again.

Lisa picked up an envelope she'd dropped near the news section of the paper. She ripped it open and pulled out the card inside. An invitation of some sort with fancy edges and printed on heavy card stock. She froze and alarm surfaced in Sam.

"Something wrong?"

"Look." She handed over the invitation for him to read.

In the center of the fancy card were the words *You have been chosen*.

"Any identification on the envelope? A postmark?" Sam sniffed it and handed the invitation over to Henry who did the same.

"There isn't a postmark. The envelope is plain." Lisa passed it to Gerard.

"No citrus aftershave," Sam said.

"No," Henry said after sniffing it again.

Sam pushed away his plate. "You need to get an alarm."

"I'll get some quotes, but the truth is I can't afford an alarm. I struggle to pay the rates and insurance as it is." Lisa lifted her chin and Sam's offer of lending her money froze on his lips.

"Okay. We could fit locks to the windows. Henry, Gerard and I can install them for you."

Lisa frowned. "I appreciate the offer, but I'm going to need to replace the window frames soon. Some of them are old and rotting, so it seems pointless to add locks now. Look, the break-in is a kid playing a prank. Mrs. Humphries, the elderly lady next door, was complaining about high school students stealing fruit off her apple trees last week. When they get together, they egg each other on. I can ask the neighbors if they saw anything out of place."

Gerard waved the invitation in front of her nose. "And this?"

"For all I know it's the start of a new advertising promotion. Businesses put all sorts of junk mail in my box. I have a pile there. Besides, while it's true the intruder freaked me out last night, I am a shifter. I'm stronger than I appear and most humans would underestimate my physical strength."

"That's not going to stop someone from hiding and creeping up on you from behind. They could hit you over the head before you knew they were there or give you a shot to knock you out," Henry said in a stern voice.

"What if I booby trap my windows? My bedroom has a lock. If I get you to put locks on the bedroom windows, would that make you happier?"

"It's a start," Henry said. "Why don't we take care of that for you before we head back to the farm?"

Sam held his breath, hoping that Lisa would do the sensible thing without him interfering.

She never hesitated. "Thank you. That would make me feel safer."

"You could always stay with me," Sam said, a burst of yearning filling him as he voiced his wish. While he wanted to drag her to his home and safety, instinctively, he knew he wouldn't win Lisa in that manner. She'd lived on her own for two years. From the little she said, the prior months had been full of looking after her husband. She made her own decisions and he couldn't take that away from her. In truth, her independent streak, her capable nature made her even more attractive. The clingy type of woman scared him enough to send him scurrying for cover.

"I have clients visiting me here."

"New clients?" Henry asked.

"Sometimes."

Sam took a calming breath and reached for his coffee while he struggled with his instinct to bark out orders. A palpable silence fell, broken by the doorbell.

Lisa rose to answer the summons.

"Make sure you know who it is before you answer the door," Henry instructed in a clipped tone.

Lisa froze, the color fleeing from her face. "Stop trying to scare me. It's probably Mrs. Humphries wanting to borrow a cup of sugar."

"Nosy neighbors are good," Gerard said.

"Not if they're frail and should know better," Lisa retorted and disappeared from the kitchen when the doorbell rang a second time.

Gerard glanced at him. "Why couldn't you pick a biddable woman?"

Sam sighed and went with the facts. "They bore me silly. I prefer a woman who thinks for herself."

Henry chewed on a mouthful of crispy bacon and swallowed. "Especially if they're like Lisa. She the one you've been hung up on for years?"

"Yeah."

Gerard glanced at the doorway and leaned closer. "So how is sex with the babysitter?"

"None of your business." Sam followed up with a growl and Gerard straightened abruptly.

"Use your nut, man," Henry said. "If the sex was crap, we wouldn't be here. He would have walked away after his weekend in Middlemarch."

Gerard eyed Sam. "True?"

"True." Sam turned toward the door as Lisa wandered back to the kitchen, her arms laden with a huge bouquet of blue, white and pink flowers. He didn't recognize most of them, but they were pretty and reminded him of his mother's rose garden. A spike of guilt struck when he thought of the state of the gardens around the house. Just as well his parents were away in America, visiting some of the feline clans and doing the tourist thing. It meant they couldn't make sneak visits to their old residence.

"Sam, thank you. They're beautiful."

Crap. Should he have done flowers? He'd never bought flowers for a woman. Never thought of it. "I wish I'd thought of the idea."

"Is there a card?" Henry asked.

She set the flowers on the kitchen counter and plucked out a small white envelope. Sam noticed her hands trembled a fraction, and he stood. He placed his arm around her waist, offering silent comfort as she opened the card.

He heard the catch of her breath even as he read the words on the card. *Congratulations. Enjoy the game.*

"What game?" Lisa asked.

"The card says, *Congratulations. Enjoy the game.* There's no name." Sam enlightened his friends.

Gerard stood and grabbed the pot of coffee. "Everyone want a refill?"

"No thanks," Lisa said.

Gerard filled the rest of the cups and returned the coffeepot to the element. "You don't know of anyone who could have sent the flowers?"

"No."

"We can question the florist," Henry said. "Who delivered them? A courier?"

"A florist truck delivered them," Lisa said. "The same name as on the bouquet." She eyed it as if it were a small creature poised to attack.

The doorbell went again.

"I'll get it." Sam paused, willing to give way if Lisa wanted to answer her own door.

"Thanks," she said. "I might eat the rest of my breakfast."

Sam strode to get the door. He wrenched it open, his feline close to the surface.

"Oh." The little old lady at the door patted her chest in the region of her heart. She came up to his chest and peered at him with curious birdlike eyes, her hair in a bun thing on top of her head. A small Jack Russell sat at her side, and on seeing Sam, the dog growled. "Is Lisa home?" She waggled a white china mug in front of his face. "I wanted to do some baking and realized I've run out of sugar. I'd hoped Lisa would lend me a cup."

Sam eyed the growling dog with caution. "Come into the kitchen." He hoped Lisa didn't mind.

"Mrs. Humphries," Lisa said. "How are you?"

The dog's claws clicked on the wooden flooring. His small body vibrated with another growl on sighting Lisa.

His black nose lifted, he sniffed, freezing mid-growl when he spotted Henry. He cocked his furry head, let out a strange whine and trotted over to Henry. He licked the werewolf's hand and dropped, stretching out at Henry's side.

Mrs. Humphries took in Gerard and Henry and patted her silver hair. "I'm so sorry to interrupt." Then she batted her eyelashes and Sam barked out a laugh, quickly stifled, at Gerard's startled expression. "Oh, Lisa. What pretty flowers. Did your beau give them to you?"

"No, they came from a client," Lisa said. "Unfortunately, there is something in the bouquet that doesn't agree with me." She coughed and backed away from the flowers. "Would you like them?"

"Oh, no. I couldn't."

"It seems a shame to waste them," Lisa said. "I'm only going to throw them away."

"My friends are coming for afternoon tea," Mrs. Humphries said and held up her white mug. "That is why I've come. Could I borrow a cup of sugar? I want to make a carrot cake."

"Of course you can," Lisa said and she took the mug and went to one of her cupboards. "I have an unopened bag," she said. "Why don't you take the whole thing and buy me a bag next time you go shopping?"

"I couldn't," Mrs. Humphries said. "I'd hate to run you short."

"I'm not going to have much time for baking this week," Lisa said.

"Well, if you're sure."

Sam bit back a grin. The elderly woman wasn't missing a thing. He'd bet she could describe each of them to her old biddy friends this afternoon. Henry caught his gaze and jerked his head toward Mrs. Humphries. Good idea, Sam thought, reading Henry's meaning with the ease of a long friendship.

Henry pushed away his empty plate and stood. "I'll carry the flowers and sugar for you and escort you home, Mrs. Humphries."

Mrs. Humphries fluttered her lashes again and gave a shy titter. "Oh, I couldn't."

"It's no trouble to escort a beautiful woman," Henry said and picked up the bouquet. The dog followed Henry, but aimed a passing growl at Sam and Lisa. In his quiet way, Henry had Mrs. Humphries organized and out the door in mere minutes.

"I wonder if she saw anything last night," Gerard said.

"We'll soon know," Sam answered with a grin. "Henry will extract the information. Do you see your neighbors on the other side or the ones opposite?"

"I wave to the business couple opposite if I see them, but both of them work long hours. The ones on the other side, I see occasionally. The trees block vision, so they wouldn't see anyone in my driveway. They'd only notice someone wandering around the garden if they happened to look out their windows. The couple have a teenage daughter. I spot her climbing out the window on occasion."

Henry returned to the kitchen. "She didn't see anyone, although she did notice a man on a motorbike stop to talk on his phone. She said he spoke for about ten minutes then drove away. She said the people opposite had a visitor last night and he didn't leave until this morning, and she wondered if you should go running on your own. Nothing wrong with her eyesight. Not much gets past her."

"What did you tell her?" Lisa asked. "I don't want her to play Miss Marple and get hurt in the process."

"I said that someone broke into your place last night," Henry said. "I told her to make sure she locks up and to take care with her security."

Lisa groaned. "She's going to be over here asking questions once you leave. Stop worrying. As I said, someone is either planning a promotion or playing a joke on me."

But Sam didn't think she believed that. The knowledge that someone had wandered around her house and touched her things had upset her, even if she was trying to hide her fear. "Even if it is a joke, it won't hurt to beef up security."

"Thanks for the breakfast, Lisa," Gerard said. "Henry and I will go to the hardware store and pick up some locks."

Lisa smiled but Sam saw the strain behind the forced curl of her lips. "Thank you."

He waited until his friends left and turned to her. "Are you okay?"

"I feel violated. This house always felt safe, felt like a haven and now it doesn't."

Sam wanted to tell her she could sell it and move in with him, but he left the words unsaid. Too soon. While he knew what he wanted, Lisa needed to get used to the idea. "We'll make it safe for you again. Stay with me a couple of nights."

"I have the awards dinner next week."

"You could invite me to stay with you after the dinner."

She smiled. "That's a great idea, but what about your morning jobs?"

"Henry and Gerard have offered to help. Everything will be fine." Sam drew her into his arms and held her close. He dragged her scent deep into his lungs and his inner angst settled to a dull throb of irritation. He'd just found Lisa again. No way would he let anyone hurt her.

Chapter 5

Flowers

E verything would turn out all right. If she let her panic escalate, her intruder would win.

Sam held her quietly for a few minutes before pulling back to kiss her forehead. "Don't worry."

"I'm probably stressing about nothing." Lisa checked her watch. "Cripes, I'd better hurry. I have a client coming in half an hour, and I need to shower."

Her phone rang, and she reached across the counter to grab it. The number wasn't familiar and she hesitated for a second. *No, this is stupid.* She answered the phone. "Hello, Lisa Jordan Design."

"You gave away my flowers?"

"What flowers?" Lisa demanded, her stomach lurching.

Sam's gaze sharpened and he gestured her to keep talking.

"You sent me flowers?" she asked.

"Tsk-tsk. I watched them arrive. I saw one of your men deliver them to the lady next door. I am most disappointed in you."

"Who is this?"

"Me?" The man laughed, a chilling sound that gripped her chest and stalled her breathing. In the next instant, her feline twisted beneath her skin, attempting to force past her human control. "Why, I'm your stalker. I look forward to getting to know you better, Lisa Jordan."

"But—" The phone clicked in her ear. An enraged feline growl rushed up her throat. "Well. It's official. That man just told me he's stalking me. Crazy!"

"I heard," Sam said. "We need to report this to the police."

"What are we going to tell them? That someone prowled around my house, touched my things and sent me flowers?"

"Yes," Sam said. "You need to get this on the record. He implied that he intended to stalk you. He stated it up front."

"He might be joking."

"And he might not," Sam countered. "I'll wait here with you until you've conducted your business, then we'll head to the nearest police station and make a formal complaint.

It's the right thing to do. Even if this man is joking, he's scaring you, and that's not right. Did you recognize his voice?"

"No, not at all."

"Don't worry. We'll sort this out. Go and have a shower. We'll do what we can with locks on the windows while you're with your client. Is it a new client or one you've worked with before? Male or female?"

"A new one. I did some work for this man's sister. She liked what I did and recommended me to her brother who runs his own garage, not far from here."

"I want to meet him. Smell him."

"No, it's all right. I'll scream if I need help."

"I'll wait with you until you meet him."

"I— All right." She speared him a look. The phone call had rattled her. "But you'll leave as soon as the introductions are done."

"Agreed."

Although Sam kept his word, he managed to appear menacing and made her client so uneasy he agreed with every one of her ideas and left after half an hour. She sighed and strode back to her desk. Sam had slipped into full bossy, alpha mode, acting as if he was her mate. They'd slept together once. Her mind went back to her weekend and heat gathered in her cheeks. Okay, not quite accurate.

Sex had occurred many times during the night and day they'd spent together, but he had no right to direct her life.

And during the drive to the police station, she intended to tell him so and give him her version of the rules.

Her rules.

They were not a couple.

This thing between them was good, hot sex—a mutual scratching of an itch—and nothing more.

Later that day, Sam's farm, outside Christchurch

"I need to do some work. Where can I set up?" Lisa asked.

"You're welcome to use my office." Sam led her through the single-level farmhouse. Although clean, most of the furnishings were old and well-worn. Probably from when his parents had lived here before they moved to a smaller place, closer to the city, prior to taking off on their overseas adventure.

"Nothing special, I know, but I've been sinking all my profits back into the farm." Sam said this without a defensive tone, merely stating facts.

"I've been doing the same thing, hence the old window frames, which require replacing, are still in use."

"Don't worry. The new locks the boys installed plus the solar security lights will put off most intruders." He led her into a surprisingly modern office with a streamlined wooden-veneer desk, an executive chair, filing cabinets and a wall covered with ribbons and awards.

Intrigued, Lisa wandered over to the nearest wall to peruse some of the framed certificates. "They're yours. I didn't know you did eventing."

"After I left school at sixteen. My mother wanted me to stay at school, do more study, but I hated it. Couldn't sit still, so I left as soon as I could. I did a short stint of rodeos when I worked at a cattle station in Australia, owned by an Australia shifter group. Then, I moved to England and got into eventing. That was before I went into the army at age twenty."

"You must have been good. Why did you give up competing? You could've gone back to it after you left the army. And why the army?" Her questions tumbled out like water over a steep rock cliff, fast and furious, because her curiosity blazed with the ferocity of a wildfire. He'd left home at such a young age. "And how long have you been back home? I never thought to ask you."

His green eyes glittered with amusement, but he never hesitated to answer her questions. "Because the work—both competing and army—took me away from home. I'd started to butt heads with my father because I thought he needed to modernize and try new methods. I enjoyed breaking and training horses. Well-schooled horses go for big money. I loved the rodeo circuit but it's hard on the body and most riders get hurt sooner or later. I was lucky with injuries. The army—" He paused to shake his head. "Henry and Gerard had decided to join so I did too, since on my return back to New Zealand, I butted heads with my father even more. The few years in the army taught me different skills. When Mum and Dad wanted to retire from farming and travel, I decided to come back to my roots. Dad still owns half the farm, and I'm paying off the loans I took out to buy the other half. Eventually, I hope to own the entire farm. We still run a few sheep, a herd of cattle, and I've built up the horses and training side. I enjoy being my own boss instead of taking orders."

Lisa had known some of this, but not all, and his matter-of-fact telling left out the hard times in between. Farming was a tough business and he'd impressed her. The army couldn't have been easy either. The man reminded her of an onion with his peeling layers of mystery. She'd assumed he'd gone straight into the army after leaving school, but he'd done other travel, other things. "Do you still butt heads with your father?"

"Let's say we've both matured a bit, and Mum keeps him busy with her latest plans for travel or crafts. He doesn't have the time to oversee me." He grinned. "I love my father, but he's not the most patient man."

Lisa remembered Mr. Mitchell, a stern feline male but putty in his wife's hands—a tiny blonde with infinite patience and excellent management skills. She'd been a real loss to the Feline Council when the family had moved north to Christchurch.

"You can use this desk. Leave your laptop set up. This is the wireless password if you need the internet." He wrote something on a piece of paper and handed it to her.

"Thanks." Her phone rang and she pulled it from the side of her computer bag. An unknown number.

"Remember what the policeman said. If you don't recognize the number, don't answer the call. Let it go to voice mail."

"And if it's a client?" She heard the combative tone in her voice and grimaced. "Sorry. I know you're trying to help."

The phone stopped ringing, then started again, and her stomach did a slow flip, her heart speeding into a flight-or-fight jungle pound.

Sam's arm went around her quivering shoulders. "Why don't you leave your phone here, and I'll give you the fifty-cent tour of the house and stables? I think I'll have a pair of gumboots to fit you."

Sam might be younger than her, but his matter-of-fact behavior calmed her racing heart and she even managed a shaky smile. "I've tried and tried to think what I might have done to piss someone off, but I can't think of a thing."

"You're a good person, Lisa. The cop said it could simply be a cruel joke or you might remind the guy of a past lover. It could be anything, so don't dwell on the reasons. Come and see my horses. Do you ride? I don't even know."

"No, and I don't intend to start. How is it that the horses don't react to your feline? Even Mrs. Humphries's dog growls at me, although he did seem to like Henry."

"Oh, they react at first, which is why I prefer to breed my own stock. They know I won't hurt them. It worked as a plus on the rodeo circuit. The bulls always bucked twice as hard and scored good points. All I did was hang on and we both looked good."

"You make it sound easy." The strident summons of the phone ceased and the steel seeped from her spine. "I'd love a tour."

Sam reached for her hand and tugged her back down the passage, through a kitchen with a few dirty cups in the sink and into a porch with an assortment of gumboots, lined up with military precision. He glanced at her feet. "I think these will fit."

She slid off her trainers and tried the right boot. "Perfect."

Seconds later, they exited the house and stepped into the warmth of an early autumn day. Grasping her hand again, Sam tugged her along a narrow path. The garden plants grew in a wild profusion along with a sprinkling of weeds. The first leaves had started to fall from the trees, and they crunched underfoot. Sam paused to open a gate and ushered her through. They followed another track, gravel and leaves beneath their boots.

While the wooden farmhouse showed its age with its shabby furnishings and peeling white paint on its exterior, the stables appeared new and sparkling clean. The scent of hay and straw and horses grew deeper and richer as they neared the first of the stables. The faint sound of a radio carried on the air, and in a room to their right, someone sang off-tune.

"Is that you, Keith?" Sam called in a tetchy voice. "The hospital said you had to rest that leg."

"I was going stir-crazy in my bedroom. Casey and Brian helped me out here. I'm cleaning tack."

Sam led her in that direction, and they entered a room that smelled of horses, leather and something else she couldn't identify. As he'd promised, Keith sat in a chair with his right leg propped up on a stool. A white cast, wrapped in plastic to protect it from dirt and water covered his leg to above the knee. Lisa had expected someone around Sam's age, but this man seemed nearer retirement, and his skin bore the weathered signs of a man who spent his days outdoors.

"What is the smell?" Lisa asked.

"Saddle soap to clean and oil to condition the leather," Sam said.

"Not me," Keith said with a sly wink.

She wrinkled her nose. "Good to hear."

"This is Lisa," Sam said. "We've known each other since we were kids."

Keith dipped his cloth in the oil and applied it to the saddle sitting on his lap. "So you'll know what a grumpy-bum he is if he doesn't get his coffee in the morning."

Lisa hid her smile and slid a sideways glance at Sam. "He's been on his best behavior so far."

"Ah, the honeymoon period," Keith teased.

Sam let out a very feline growl and Keith never blinked, yet Lisa knew he was human and not shifter.

"See?" Keith said. "It must be time for his afternoon cup."

Sam tugged on Lisa's hand. "I would fire him," he said. "But I inherited him with the farm. He refuses to leave."

Lisa gave a little wave with her free hand. "Nice to meet you, Keith. Look after that leg."

"Call me when you're ready to go back to your house," Sam said to Keith. "I'll give you a hand."

"Sure thing, boss."

Sam kept his grip on her hand as he led her deeper into the stables. A horse whickered in greeting and stuck its chestnut head over a stall door.

"This is Jessie. I'll take her out in a few minutes for a training run." Sam dropped Lisa's hand and approached the stall. After grabbing a bridle off a hook, he opened the stall and slipped inside. He crooned to the horse and petted her before slipping on the bridle with practiced ease. "I have a buyer coming to see her tomorrow."

"You're selling her?" Lisa asked in surprise because it was obvious to her how much Sam loved this horse.

"I have a loan payment coming up," he said. "I've always known I'd have to sell her, even though she's such a sweetheart. I get attached to all my horses, but I decide early on which ones I need to sell and at which stage of the training process."

"That must be hard."

"It is, but this is a business. I think of the horses I sell as advertising, and I vet the purchasers."

Lisa stepped out of the way when Sam led Jessie from the stall. The rest of the stalls seemed to be empty. "Where are the other horses? You do have more, right?"

"Yes. They're all out in the paddocks. Jessie will join them once we finish our training session. We use the stables during the colder weather or if a mare is foaling."

"What sort of training are you doing? Can I watch?"

"I'll take her through a warm-up and practice some of the dressage steps I've been teaching her. She loves to jump, so we'll run a few as a treat."

Sam led Jessie toward the room where Keith had set up.

"Here. Hold the reins for me while I grab a saddle." He gave her the reins and disappeared before she could reply.

Jessie stepped closer and nuzzled her hair, not bothered by a stranger or her feline scent.

"What a beautiful girl you are," Lisa whispered and stroked her hand along the glossy neck.

"My two favorite girls together," Sam said with a smile as he reappeared with a saddle blanket and saddle.

Watching Sam at work fascinated her, and Lisa enjoyed sitting on the rails of the fence while he put Jessie through her paces. This was a different side of Sam. He was confident and patient and praised the horse often. The rapport between them shone through, and Lisa wondered how he could bear to sell the horse.

From where she sat, she could see horses grazing in the nearby paddocks. Farther away, the flat paddocks gave way to rolling hills, full of grazing sheep. The sun shone down and the neigh of a horse carried on the air. A bird sang from a rustling karaka tree and each breath she inhaled carried the scent of horses and grass. The countryside. It seemed so quiet after the bombardment of civilization in the city.

Thoughts of the city led to her house and the renewed security measures. The cop they'd spoken to had told them they couldn't do anything unless the stalker escalated his actions and committed a crime or if he approached her directly. Lisa sucked in a quick breath. God, she hated this feeling of someone watching her, loathed the idea that someone had trespassed on her privacy and touched her things. Her home had always felt safe, and now she jumped at shadows.

"Hi, you must be Lisa."

Lisa turned to see a teenage girl standing behind her. She wore jeans and a T-shirt under an olive-green coat with sturdy boots on her feet. A black cap covered her thick blonde hair. "I am."

"I'm Casey. I've just come to tell you that Brian and I are taking Uncle Keith back to his house. Can you tell Sam? Oh, and tell him we've finished all the chores on his list for today. The sheep are in the new paddock and the water is fine."

"Will do," Lisa said.

Casey cocked her head. "You're just as pretty as Sam said."

"Sam discussed me?"

"A long time ago. I asked him why he never got serious about any of the women he dated." She glanced into the training arena before continuing. "He said he'd met the woman he wanted to marry but the stars weren't aligned yet."

"Me?"

"Yeah, he told me your name."

"Oh." Lisa lost the power of speech. Sam had been waiting for *her*?

Casey raised a hand in farewell. "Catch you later." And seconds later, she had disappeared, leaving Lisa alone with her confusion. Sam had wanted her all these years? It couldn't be the truth, could it?

Chapter 6

Sam and Sweet Dreams

Later that night

S am drew her into his bedroom. "I've dreamed about having you in my bed." He started to say more but stopped, and Lisa thought again of Casey's words.

She'd married David, not long after leaving Middlemarch. How had...

"Stop thinking so hard. You'll get old and wrinkled," Sam teased.

"Thank you for today, for suggesting I come with you."

"Did you get your work done? Everything you needed to do?"

"I did. I feel as if I should have cooked dinner since I spent the afternoon lazing around."

"Ah, but you weren't lazing. You were watching me and getting inspiration for the job you're working on."

"I think my client will be pleased," she said.

"I should get my reward now," Sam said, his green eyes twinkling.

Such a handsome man. He'd certainly grown into the promise he'd shown as a youngster. The thought gave her pause, made her feel like a dirty old woman again.

"I'll just get comfortable," Sam said and whipped his black T-shirt over his head to display a broad, muscled chest. Nothing young about that sexy body. He unfastened his jeans—the pair he'd changed into after doing the last of his farm chores—and drew them down his hips, taking his boxer-briefs with them. Slim hips. Muscular thighs. Unbidden her gaze drifted to his groin and heat flooded her torso and swept upward in a dizzying rush. Nothing young or immature about Sam Mitchell.

"I enjoy you looking at me." His gritty tone drew her gaze, and she saw his eyes glowed with an inner feline light. He didn't try to hide his desire for her. "I like knowing you see me as a man."

"It's taken time," she said, giving him honesty. "I—this is going to sound weird, but I feel loyalty to my husband even though he's not here any longer."

Sam crossed the space separating them and took hold of both her hands. He met her gaze unflinchingly, and she saw banked longing and infinite patience. Casey's words floated through her mind and she began to believe. Sam *had* wanted her for a long time.

"You loved him. I understand that. From what I heard, he was a good man, a decent man."

"Yes." Lisa took a deep breath and realized she wasn't being fair to Sam. "You're the first man I've wanted, the only one I've slept with since I've been alone. I-I like you a lot."

"I know, sweetheart. Otherwise, we wouldn't have spent the weekend together and you wouldn't be here now. Tell me I have a chance, Lisa. I deserve that much."

"I wouldn't be here if I didn't care for you," Lisa said, his husky endearment—also David's for her—punching heat and longing to life. Old and yet new. *Perfect.* "I could have gone to a hotel and been safe. Instead, I came with you."

"You can sleep in one of the spare rooms if you want."

"I'm right where I want to be. I'm going to say this because it needs saying. I loved David with everything I had, but I also promised him I'd keep living and if I found someone else to make me happy, I'd move on. It's time for me to move on with you. I want to see where we go and if we mesh."

His smile—when it came—almost blinded her. It started slow, an unhurried curve at the corners of his mouth, then it spread across his face, finally reaching his eyes and lighting up his features with happiness. It made her glad she'd bared her heart.

"So you're not hung up about the age difference?"

"We haven't run out of conversation during the time we've spent together, we're both felines, and I haven't discovered any bad habits that might put me off. All of that is more important than an age gap."

"Keith is right. I am a grumpy-bum if I don't have coffee in the morning."

"Stubbornness is my middle name. Just ask my sister."

"You have taken a long time to confess you might be interested in me," he conceded.

Her hands went to the buttons on her shirt. "None of us is perfect. It would be a boring world if we were."

"True." His gaze followed her fingers as she slipped the buttons running down the front of her pale blue shirt free, one by one, to reveal her lacy white bra.

"You are gorgeous."

A streak of shyness hit since her body wasn't as perky as it used to be in her teens. Then, she shoved aside the insecurity because the way Sam looked at her brought a rash of pleasure. He saw her differently. His right hand trembled a fraction as he reached for her shirt, and that small show of nerves quieted her own anxiety.

Lisa watched him, saw his pleasure, his enjoyment, his awe. "You make me feel special."

"You are special. I can't wait to touch your breasts, to drag in your beautiful scent and to love you with my mouth. I love the taste of you and the small noises you make at the back of your throat just before you come."

Invisible energy sizzled across her skin, gravity dropping it downward until it coalesced between her thighs. Pleasure. So much pleasure. Sam seemed to read her mind, to know what or how to touch her to edge up her enjoyment. She went mushy inside as he unhooked her bra and slid the straps down her arms. He brushed a quick kiss across the curve of one breast and her breath caught, her heart attempting to hammer from her chest.

"I wanted to go slow. I can't." And he started to help with the rest of her clothes, removing them with practiced ease. She shoved aside the murmurs of jealousy seeping into her brain because she had no right. She'd been married. They both brought baggage with them to this new relationship.

He provided balance while she shimmied out of her tight jeans. Her matching lacy white underwear ripped free, aided by a quick tug from Sam.

"They look expensive but they were in the way. I will buy you more."

"Maybe I should go commando."

He glanced up with a smile. "Would you do that—at least while we're at home. It would be so convenient."

She felt her brows rise, experienced another of those whooshes of heat. This one frisked her breasts and dive-bombed her pussy. "Are you intending to grab me often?"

"Yes," he said bluntly. "One look at your sexy arse and I'm hungry for you. I don't think I'll ever get enough."

An "oh" formed on her lips but didn't emerge because he lifted her in one quick, easy action and tossed her on the king-size bed. Before she stopped bouncing, he had his head between her thighs and he licked a path down her slit.

"You taste good," he whispered, each word puffing warm air against her flesh. He pushed her hard and fast, swirling pleasure through her with each lap of his tongue and pull of his lips. Her thighs quivered, and she gripped the cotton duvet cover in an effort to anchor herself. But he didn't allow her a respite. He pushed her up fast with each tender caress of her clit. He added his fingers to good effect, alternating licks and strokes until she quivered like an autumn leaf in a breeze. Pleasure detonated in her and the moan she'd attempted to stem rushed through her in concert.

She was still trembling inside and out when Sam rose and guided his cock to her entrance. The friction of his shaft sent another series of spasms through her channel, the sense of fullness so, so good.

"Harder, Sam. Harder."

He began stroking in and out of her with seamless thrusts. His easy strength thrilled her, the pleasure on his face forcing her to accept her growing feelings for him. They'd found each other mere days ago, yet it felt as if they'd known each other forever. Her feline twisted beneath her skin and the urge to bite Sam tore through her. It shocked her and she gasped, hiding her face against Sam's shoulder. He groaned and came, his big body shuddering within her embrace.

Her feline never...she had never...biting?

Something to consider later when she found herself alone.

Her phone rang a summons from the other side of the room and Sam pulled free of her.

"It might be Janice. She sometimes rings me in the evening."

"I'll answer it," he said. "Then, I'll turn it off for the night."

"Okay, but bring it over here so I can hear. If it is him, I want to listen to his voice again. I know the cops said not to engage, but maybe I'll hear something familiar, something I can place. Hearing it again might jog my memory."

Sam strode across the room and picked up her phone off the dresser. He waited until he reached her side before he answered, knowing she'd hear the other end of the call with her feline hearing. "Yes."

"Is this Lisa Jordan's phone?"

It *was* him.

Her self-professed stalker.

"Who is this?"

"What is she doing?" Sharp irritation laced the voice. "She isn't at home."

Sam glanced at her and she shook her head. "Don't ring this number again." He hung up and turned off the phone. "You didn't recognize the voice?"

"No. I deal with a lot of different people with my job. He's probably pissed off that he couldn't talk to me."

"Not your problem. Maybe you should limit your client conversation to email at present and record your incoming calls. That way you'd have something physical to show the cops if he uses that method of communication."

Lisa thought about the idea and nodded. "I can do that. Even if I have to explain I have a stalker, my clients would understand."

"Good. Let's push the bastard from our minds and get to more pleasant things."

"Again? Already?"

"A side benefit of a younger man. We have quick recuperation powers."

Lisa let her gaze sweep down his sexy bod and skim his groin. As she studied him, his erection grew larger, and she grinned. "Could be fun."

His countenance held wickedness and promise along with a good serving of lust. "It will be. I promise."

The following week

Lisa smiled as she climbed from her car and headed for Sam's house. A successful client meeting and just a couple of phone calls featuring heavy breathing. She might even go home tonight. It would be easier since she had a busy day tomorrow then had the awards dinner.

Sam wasn't at the house, but he'd said he might be running late because he had a second buyer coming to see his horse—Jessie—and to wait for him. They intended to run together in feline form, and she couldn't wait to embrace this side of her psyche again with a man she cared for—Sam. A shudder of pleasure worked through her at the idea of running and sparring together as leopards again. The run in Middlemarch had been fun and it was a treat to repeat the experience again when she didn't run in feline form often, making do with her morning runs, done in the normal human way.

Deep in thought, she collided with the bulk in front of her.

"Ah, beautiful Lisa." Henry wrapped his arms around her to halt a fall. "Are you free Friday night? Come out to dinner with me."

"Thanks, but no. That would make Sam unhappy." Henry scored a rating of gorgeous in a stern werewolf kind of way, but he wasn't Sam.

Henry shrugged without concern. "If you change your mind, you know where to find me."

"Nah, she'd prefer a feline. Right, Lisa," Gerard said, appearing from the direction of the stable block.

"Yes, I would. Sam," she said with a grin. She stepped away from Henry. "Did you see anything weird last night when you stayed at my place?"

Both Henry and Gerard quit with their teasing, going serious. "Nothing we could see or hear. Mrs. Humphries walked her dog a few times. She came to the door and wanted to know what we were doing."

"What did you tell her?"

"That you were letting us stay for a few days. Sam said you had a phone call."

"Yeah. I've been vetting my calls, recording them and answering the ones from numbers I recognize."

Henry nodded. "Best not to engage."

"Have you seen Sam?"

"He's still at the stables."

"Thanks." Lisa lifted her hand in farewell and strode to the stable block, anxious to meet Sam. Janice was right. The seven years between them offered no barrier.

Lisa found him showing Jessie and speaking to the female buyer when she arrived, so she hung back, content to watch until he'd finished. Sam returned the horse to the stable. Lisa started to approach the couple when the woman walked into Sam's arms and they kissed.

Lisa jammed her hand against her mouth to halt her croak of protest. Betrayal cut like a dagger to her heart.

Tears welled and she realized she'd fallen for Sam. Hard. Which was why witnessing his duplicity hurt so much. Stumbling, she turned to flee, glad she'd discovered his disloyalty before telling him she wanted more from their relationship.

Wait!

Lisa froze at the stern voice. David hadn't spoken to her much recently, and while part of her missed the connection, she understood. She'd moved on while David remained rooted in the past.

Turn around and watch them. Now.

Slowly Lisa turned, steeling her heart against the pain of seeing Sam embrace someone else. She took half a step in retreat.

Sam's friend had his hands all over you earlier. To an outsider, it might have appeared as if you were willing but you and I know better.

This time when Lisa turned to watch, she was better prepared. She studied the nuances and realized what David meant. The woman clung to Sam while Sam pushed at her shoulders. He didn't want her kiss. Buoyed by the realization, she stepped closer.

"Damn, Katrina. How many times do I have to tell you? Not interested," Sam snapped.

"That's right," Lisa said. "Because he has all the woman he can handle with me."

"Lisa." Sam appeared apprehensive while she approached, until she winked at him.

She stood on tiptoe to kiss his cheek. "Almost done?"

"Katrina, what have you decided about the horse?"

The woman scowled in an unattractive manner. "Yeah. Not worth the price you're asking."

"It's a fair price for a horse of her caliber."

Katrina shrugged one shoulder. "Call me if you want to negotiate." She sauntered off with a twitch of her jeans-clad ass.

Sam turned to her with a troubled frown. "Lisa, I didn't kiss—"

She slapped fingers over his mouth. "I know. I saw you weren't an eager participant. Although you could have pushed her a bit harder and made her end up on the ground on her man-stealing arse. You ready to go for a run?" She stepped away but watched him expectantly.

"As soon as I make sure Katrina has gone. Why is Henry's scent on you?"

"I crashed right into him, not looking where I was going."

Sam growled deep in his throat. "He didn't have to cop a feel at the same time."

Fifteen minutes later, they stood at the edge of a stand of trees. Rolling hills stretched out to Lisa's right while to her left the Canterbury plains extended into the distance, reminding her of a living patchwork quilt with green paddocks, crops of different hues, and cultivated fields making up the squares.

"Are you ready?" Sam asked, a twinkle in his green eyes.

"More than ready to run off some stress."

"No more phone calls from strange men wanting to buy a night with Saucy Lisa?"

Lisa snorted. "They seemed to have trailed off. Thank god. Just a couple of calls with heavy breathing. No flowers or intruders. I don't know if it's my imagination, but I feel as if someone is watching me whenever I leave the house for work or to run errands. I never see anyone. I don't think anyone followed me here."

"Don't worry. My security is excellent. I beefed it up after some of our sheep disappeared. No one will get close without me or my staff knowing."

"Good." With a carefree laugh, she started tearing off her clothes. Footwear flew through the air, clothes dropped to the ground and finally she was naked.

Lisa called her feline in her mind, embracing the pain of the shift as muscles twisted, bones lengthened and black fur rushed across her skin. She loped away, glorying in her enhanced senses—the scent of the grasses and soil, the green aroma from the trees, the sharp call of a bird hidden somewhere in the nearby hedge.

As Sam raced up behind her, she increased her speed, tearing across the ground, luxuriating in the play of muscles. He leaped at her and they tumbled in a pile, mock snarling and testing their strength against each other.

Finally, Sam nudged her to the right and in minutes, she found herself overlooking a pond. The sun shone over the surface, making it glint and sparkle. Lisa followed and they entered a private, grassy spot with views over the pond. After prowling over to her, he rubbed against her shoulder, nudged her head and licked her muzzle with a rasp of his tongue. He made a handsome cat, bigger than her, solid and muscular. She trembled with need, her purrs of pleasure halting abruptly when he retreated.

He shifted, rolling smoothly to his feet to stare down at her. "Shift."

Her heart started to beat a little faster and desire sprang through her body. Awareness rippled between them as she studied his beautiful, muscular form. *Hers*. She laughed softly to herself, her thoughts holding mockery. It hadn't taken her long to decide that maybe the seven years between them weren't important. Sam wasn't a man who jumped from bed to bed or at least, he didn't now. She hadn't found any evidence of a female at his house.

"Lisa." His tone held command, and everything feminine in her tightened in excitement.

She closed her eyes, took a deep breath and pictured her human form. She let the change take her and stood to face him.

"You are so beautiful. I can't make up my mind where I want to touch you first."

"No problem." She found herself grinning at him. "I'll do the touching." And she closed the distance between them. Warm skin greeted her questing fingers as she smoothed them over his pectoral muscles. She slid one hand behind him and down his back. Her quick pinch of his butt had him jumping. A growl escaped him and her amusement at her sly move peeled out in laughter.

"Think you're clever, don't you?" he growled and seconds later, he swung her into his arms and gave her a quick kiss, over way too fast. "I missed you today."

Pleased surprise filled her because she'd missed him too. Several times during the day, she went to call him, to tell him something, to repeat the joke from the radio that still made her chuckle when she thought of the punchline. "I missed you too."

"You could move in with me." He set her down on a soft, grassy patch and caged her with his bigger body.

"But it hasn't been long since we met again in Middlemarch." She relaxed and smiled up at him, letting her happiness free.

He brushed a lock of hair off her cheek. "It's long enough for me to know what I want."

She frowned and struggled to find the right words. They failed to come and frustration filled her. "I—"

He placed a hand over her mouth. "No, it's all right. I understand this is a big decision for you and you need more time. I'm fine with that as long as I know that we're at least on the same page. Are we? On the same page?"

Relief flooded her. "We are. I want to see where this thing between us will go."

"So, you won't date any other men?"

"No, and I'd better not find you flirting with other women. I won't be responsible for my actions."

The corners of his eyes crinkled. "Deal. Let's kiss to seal our promises."

She fluttered her eyelashes at him. "I hope we're going to do more than kiss."

"Baggage."

Before she could reply, his lips halted further conversation and he didn't muck around, his kiss one of determination and seduction. Her arms crept around his neck and she held him tight, melting under his sensual heat. Desire and excitement beat at her, a craving to bite springing into her mind with a suddenness that left her dizzy. She waited for David, the voice of calmness to soothe her and tell her she should continue with caution. The voices in her head remained silent.

"Hey, where did you go?"

"Nowhere," she fibbed. "I'm right here, waiting anxiously for your next move."

"My next move might send you running for the hills. I might shock your elderly mind with my licentious ways."

Laughter burst from her, dragging her back into the moment. "Let me explore you." She attempted to roll him off her but he remained in place with little effort.

"My turn."

"It's always your turn."

"Deal with it." And he proceeded to drive her crazy with his sensual strokes and well-timed pinches. Her shoulders. Her stomach. Her neck. Her skin sizzled with awareness and her breasts ached for his attention. Liquid heat readied her for his possession, but still he teased her with his caresses.

"Sam." His name was both a protest and a plea.

"Are you ready for me?"

"Yes."

He moved his attention to her breasts, taking a series of small bites from the plump curves. A groan escaped her, the pleasure growing, growing, growing with each of his touches. Then, he took one nipple into his warm mouth. He sucked hard and sensation rippled down her torso to her pussy.

"Sam, please."

"Sam, what?" he teased. "Should I stop?"

She gripped his ears and tugged. "Don't you dare."

Laughing, he evaded her hands and imprisoned them at her sides while he played with her breasts, using his mouth to good effect. Blood roared to her face and pooled between her thighs in a swooping sensation.

"Up on your hands and knees."

She stared at him for an instant, the knowledge that this was the favored position in which a male marked his mate.

"I won't bite you," he promised. "I've behaved each time we've made love. Please, I need this."

Lisa stared at him and found herself nodding even though her brain screeched to an appalled halt. It was true. He *had* behaved when he'd made the request before, but still, lectures from her mother during her teenage years jumped to the fore. *Never let a feline male take you in the mating position unless you're serious about him. This position makes a feline woman vulnerable. Make sure you love the feline before you offer consent.*

Sam studied her, his green eyes somber. He gave a chance to object and when she didn't speak, he moved off her. Her pulse rate sped like a feline sprinting for its life. Her throat ached, but she knew she could speak if she wanted, knew she could refuse and Sam wouldn't sulk. He knew this request was a big deal.

What did she do?

The silence stretched between them, pregnant with unspoken thoughts and promises. She swallowed and found herself rolling to her side and presenting her back to him. He made a sound, a tiny noise of protest, but she still remained silent. Slowly, slowly she raised her body until she knelt on all fours. Her stomach quivered and a tremor went through her. Sam sighed and her unease changed up a gear. What the hell was she doing? Move, she told herself. But she remained in place, every sense screaming in awareness. Over to her right a sheep bleated and somewhere behind them, a pheasant called its distinctive cry.

Sam's hand drifted across her back and she started.

"Lisa." Emotion shimmered in her name, but it did nothing to quieten the anxiety gripping her body and mind.

He stroked her flanks and placed a kiss in the small of her back. His abrasive tongue dragged across her back and some of the tension left her limbs. He moved closer, his breathing heavy and labored against her back. Then, his heat surrounded her, and she felt the prod of his erection at her entrance. He slid into her channel without difficulty, filling her with a new urgency.

It felt so good. So addictive. So right.

He pulled back and groaned, the throaty, masculine sound echoing around them. He sighed as he filled her again, and her apprehension receded, replaced by pleasure. He thrust and withdrew a few more times, keeping each stroke leisurely and unhurried. With each thrust, he hit a spot deep inside her that drove her crazy.

"This feels amazing. Each time seems better." His voice was low and gritty with an underpinning of feline.

"Yes," she whispered.

His tongue rasped over her shoulder blade as he pulled out to the tip. And when he stroked back inside her, his warm breath heated her neck. The fleshy pad of skin where felines bit each other to formalize their mating throbbed, and his breath felt like a brand. She hadn't known. David had touched her intimately but she'd never felt this way, as if she might detonate at his next touch.

Sam increased the pace of his strokes, their flesh slapping together now. With each impalement, his breath wafted across her mating site. His tongue lashed out, hitting her neck and a jolt of answered pleasure darted from her pussy. The beginning of her orgasm floated over her senses, but instead of pulsing to greater heights, it hovered. Her breath came in choppy gasps, air sucked into her lungs and pressed out.

"Yes," Sam whispered and his strokes became harder, erratic. His tongue licked her mating spot, his warm breath an added stimulation. Her orgasm grew and grew and grew until she wondered if her body could contain that much pleasure.

Sam grunted and she felt the deep contraction as he released. His tongue swept across the base of her neck, his hot breath bathed her skin, and she exploded. Hard, forceful jolts rippled through her pussy and darted down her legs and up her torso. She fell forward, her arms no longer willing to support her weight. For blissful seconds, Sam's weight held her down, his heated breath teasing the tender skin of her throat.

He'd kept his promise, yet a tinge of disappointment battered her pleasure-soaked mind.

The moment in time she truly believed in fated mates and second chances and pleasure too much for a body to contain.

Chapter 7

The Awards Dinner

"I'm looking forward to the dinner," Sam said as they drove into the forecourt of the swish Marion Hotel where the function took place each year.

"You want to listen to boring speeches?" She'd tried to contact James twice. Unable to catch him, she'd ended up leaving a message to tell him she'd decided to bring a date after all.

"I'll enjoy seeing you in your world. You've seen me in mine," Sam said.

Lisa shrugged. "I doubt I'll win."

"It doesn't matter. The nomination has already drawn attention to your design company. You said you've received lots of inquiries via your website. I get to see you in a sexy red dress and score a free dinner. Win-win."

"You realize they serve rubber chicken at these gigs."

Sam barked out a laugh. "I bet it has a very expensive and posh-sounding sauce. That makes it worth the suffering."

"All right, then," Lisa said. "Let's do this thing, but don't say you weren't warned."

"Wait there. I'll get your door."

Lisa hitched her black evening bag over her shoulder and waited while Sam climbed from his SUV and handed his keys over to the valet. Handsome in his charcoal-gray suit, he strode around the front of his vehicle and opened her door for her.

Arm in arm, they wandered up the red carpet of the private ballroom and she gave their invitations to the doorman. Last year, she'd attended the dinner on her own, and she'd found the pomp and ceremony—the way they announced the arrivals—a trifle off-putting. With Sam at her side, it wasn't so bad.

"Ms. Lisa Jordan and escort," the doorman announced in a deep and carrying voice.

The previous year she'd hovered indecisively and the conversation and chatter of the other attendees had scarcely abated. This year, the conversation cut and everyone in the packed ballroom turned to stare at them.

Lisa froze until Sam's arm slid around her waist.

"Which table are we sitting at?" he asked the doorman.

The doorman consulted his chart and gestured to the left. "Number ten toward the front."

Great. "Am I suffering from a wardrobe malfunction?" Lisa whispered.

"You look beautiful. Let's find our table." He guided her around the edge of the dance floor.

The silence continued for a fraction longer, then the whispering started. Lisa caught the odd word but none of the talk made sense. *Is that her? She looks okay. Who told you that? Do you think so?*

"Who are they annihilating with their gossip?" Sam asked. "Someone over to my right just asked his friend if one thousand dollars would be enough to buy a night with her."

"I've no idea," Lisa said. "That's our table there. That's strange. Why is it empty? All the other tables are full of people."

"There was a queue of cars behind us," Sam said. "Maybe the rest of our dining companions are fashionably late too."

"Sam, I have to look them in the face. I'll want to laugh if all I can think about is sex."

"It was a quickie."

"But it made us late."

"We had fun," he countered.

She couldn't argue with that, and a smile broke out at the memory.

"I knew it." Sam pulled out a chair and waited while she seated herself.

They say she offered sex, and that's how she received her nomination.

Is that true?

I've no idea, but it certainly makes for good gossip.

Lisa relaxed a fraction, since she knew they couldn't be talking about her. Not that that made the gossip right because no one deserved this sort of character assassination.

She is very good at designing. I believe she worked for a firm in Auckland.

No, I heard Dunedin.

Someone told me Wellington, another man said.

"Is this amount of gossip normal?" Sam asked, a note of distaste in his words.

"I didn't notice it last year, but I attended on my own. I feel sorry for the poor woman they're talking about."

Two couples arrived at their table, and Lisa smiled politely.

"Lisa," James said. "Good, my secretary managed to seat us at the same table. This is Sydney, my date. Sydney, this is Lisa and..." He glanced at Sam in askance.

"James, I'd like you to meet Sam."

"Ooh," Sydney purred. "A younger man. How delicious."

Tension slid through Lisa as she maintained a bland smile. What did that mean? She and Sam didn't look that far apart in age. It was her own hang-ups about being Sam's babysitter that had concerned her more than the age gap. Felines were long-lived compared to humans. Barring accidents, both she and Sam should live at least thirty years longer than the average human.

Sam reached for her hand beneath the table and squeezed her fingers. "Pleased to meet you. Are you nominated for awards tonight?"

"Yes." James's expression held a hint of chiding. "Lisa and I are nominated in the same category."

She didn't recognize the couple with James, and they did not introduce themselves. In the end, she thrust her hand at the male of the couple and said, "Hello, Lisa Jordan." She gestured at Sam. "This is my friend, Sam Mitchell."

The man gave a curt nod and turned to his partner in a full-out snub. Lisa froze, upset at the edgy atmosphere at their table. It seemed to ripple through the ballroom and bounce back in an uncomfortable intensity. Even James seemed to be acting weirdly.

Music started and several couples moved to the dance floor.

"Let's dance," Sam said, and she welcomed the interruption.

She slipped the strap of her evening bag over her shoulder, stood and walked to the dance floor with Sam at her side.

"Don't let them get to you," Sam said. "They're rude and obnoxious. We can survive a few hours."

"Thank you." She slipped into his arms and allowed herself to lean into him for a few seconds.

They danced silently, comfortable together and the tension flowed from Lisa. Sam was right. Just a few hours, then they could leave and laugh about the experience together.

"The last couple has arrived at our table," Sam murmured. "They don't look very happy."

"Why? What is wrong with everyone tonight?"

"I can't even blame it on the full moon," Sam said.

The music ended and Lisa steeled herself to return to the table.

"You're Lisa Jordan," the newly arrived woman spat.

Lisa blinked at the vehemence of the woman's tone. She had no idea of her identity and had no idea what she'd done to incur her hostility.

"You're her," the woman repeated.

"Yes."

Sam seated her and took his seat beside her. His hand reached for hers in silent commiseration.

"You should be ashamed of yourself," her companion said.

Confusion filled Lisa, and she turned to James in bewilderment. "What are they talking about? What have I done?"

"What is your going rate?" the man who'd ignored her initial greeting demanded.

"I charge standard industry rates," Lisa said. "If you're interested in a quote, you'll need to contact me via my website. I can give you a business card." She opened her small clutch bag to retrieve one.

"God, she didn't even deny it," the man's dinner companion said.

"What? Why would I?" This evening was becoming weirder by the minute.

"I believe I had a lucky escape," James said to Sydney.

Lisa found herself gaping. A lucky escape? Did he mean their date?

The four-piece band played a quick jaunty conversation breaker and the chatter died as a man in a black tuxedo approached the dais at the front of the ballroom.

"We're going to dispense with the start of our program tonight, since something unexpected and totally unacceptable has come to our attention," the man said.

Heads turned in her direction. *People were staring at her.* Sam's grip tightened around her fingers. The weirdness of the evening wasn't her imagination.

The man on the dais continued in a pompous voice. "One of the nominees in the best graphic design for the year category copied her design, taking credit for the work of others. The Design Awards committee met this afternoon for urgent consultation. We decided Lisa Jordan is hereby disqualified from the best graphic design category. We are also giving her a life disqualification from the Design Association."

Lisa gasped, shock making her shoulders slump. Then, she bounded to her feet. "What are you talking about? My design is an original."

Two security men appeared beside her.

"Please escort Ms. Jordan from the ballroom," the emcee said. "The committee has asked me to read the following statement."

Sam rose and slipped an arm around her waist. "Come on, sweetheart. This isn't the place to sort out the confusion. We'll do it tomorrow."

"But I didn't do anything wrong."

"I'm positive you didn't," he whispered. "We'll sort it out tomorrow, once we have more facts at our disposal."

His advice made sense and she lifted her head and let Sam escort her from the ballroom. The two security men trailed them, as did the whispers and excited chatter.

"My god," a woman said in disgust. "I'd heard she offered sex in exchange for contracts, but this is even worse."

Lisa's steps slowed and she glowered at the woman.

"Women like you give the rest of us a bad name," another woman shouted.

Agreement rose like the swell of a wave and Sam had to propel her the remaining distance to the exit. Her inner feline hissed and spat and she felt the beginning stages of her shift—the push of claws beneath her fingernails and the expansion of her canines. She trembled violently.

The doorman held one of the double doors open and closed it once they and the security men exited.

It was a tension-filled silence while Sam handed over his valet ticket, and they waited for their vehicle. The security men remained watchful, and Lisa's feline growled at the threat.

"Shush," Sam said in an undertone.

The SUV pulled up in front of them, and Sam escorted her to the passenger side. A few minutes later, Sam pulled away from the hotel.

"I don't understand," Lisa burst out, her hands gripped tightly in her lap. "I don't understand any of this. All of my work is original. I've never copied anyone." And the other charges of using sex to get ahead with her business. Surely people didn't believe that. She hadn't slept with anyone apart from Sam since David's death.

"Tomorrow. We'll try to discover who brought the charges against you and what evidence they have. Henry and Gerard will be able to help."

"I haven't slept with anyone apart from you. No one since David died."

Sam took one hand off the steering wheel and squeezed her knee. "I know. It's not in you to do business that way. You want to stay at the farm tonight or at your place?"

"I...my place. I'll have to start contacting my clients tomorrow. I need to go into damage control." Hopefully, it wasn't too late.

The next morning

Lisa woke him with her tossing and turning, her whimpers.

He lifted his head to ascertain the time, sighing with resignation. Early.

Sam climbed from the king-size bed and padded from Lisa's bedroom.

These accusations had knocked her, put Lisa off her normal steady equilibrium. On the ground floor, he headed for the kitchen where he found Henry and Gerard seated at the breakfast bar.

"Lisa's computer has been hacked," Gerard said. "They've screwed with her files."

"Crap." Sam reached for an empty mug and filled it with coffee. "This gets better and better. Do you think the stalker, the fiasco last night and the hacking is linked."

"It could just be bad luck," Henry said, "but my gut says it's connected. Maybe the stalker is jealous of her having a relationship with another man. Or maybe he woke up on the wrong side of the bed."

"Or maybe he disliked the color of the dress she wore last night." Sam muttered a curse. "Yeah, I get it. So how do we fix this?"

"It's a waiting game. We can't do anything until Lisa's stalker makes a move," Henry said.

"And meantime, Lisa's reputation takes a hit," Sam said.

"We'll attempt to clear her name but with all her files corrupted, it might be difficult," Gerard said.

"My files?" Lisa said from the doorway. "What's wrong with my files?"

Sam rose and went to her, his heart twisting at the stark fear on her face. "Sweetheart, someone hacked your computer and messed with your client files."

"Do you have a backup?" Henry asked.

"Yes, I back up to an external hard drive and also backup to the cloud," Lisa said. "Someone got into my computer?"

"Yes."

Sam gave her a quick hug and pushed her away. "We'll fix this. Somehow, we'll fix this for you."

"I have hard copies of most of my designs too."

"Good girl," Henry said with clear approval. "We'll document this for the police and update them with everything that has happened. Have you heard from the stalker during the last twelve hours? Has he attempted to ring you?"

"I've kept my phone turned off," she confessed.

"Maybe it's time to switch it on again," Sam said. "We need to give this guy enough rope to hang himself."

"I need to go for a run," Lisa said without warning.

"No, it's not..." Sam broke off after taking a close look at her expression. Brittle and strung tight came to mind and a wave of sympathy filled him. He'd loathe the trapped-animal sensation too. "Would you like company?"

"As long as you don't talk. Do you have shoes?"

"You can borrow mine," Gerard said.

Sam gave a nod and followed Gerard upstairs to a spare bedroom. Uneasy and unsure of what to do, Sam strode to the window and glanced outside. A motorbike was parked outside, the rider poised astride with his phone out. "Gerard, you seen this guy before? It could be innocent, but Mrs. Humphries mentioned a guy on a bike."

"I haven't noticed him before."

"Wait. Mrs. Humphries is going out for a walk with that stupid dog of hers," Gerard said. "Thing keeps growling at me."

Sam watched the elderly lady—surprisingly spry—march in the direction of the biker. Her white-and-black dog barked at the biker. Mrs. Humphries said something to the person—difficult to tell the sex from this distance—and the biker stuffed their phone inside their leather jacket. Seconds later, the bike roared to life and the rider took off with Mrs. Humphries staring after him. She said something to her dog and led him toward an oak tree, where he lifted his leg. Then, the pair trotted back up their driveway and disappeared into their brick house.

"Henry and I have been keeping watch, and we haven't seen any repeat vehicles or people strolling around the block—none that don't have a right to be in this street." Gerard handed him a pair of shoes and socks.

"Thanks for watching." Sam pulled on the socks, laced the shoes and stood. "I appreciate this."

"You've got a good woman there, and she doesn't deserve this crap falling around her head. Besides, nothing better to do. We're still looking for the right premises for our security company."

"Maybe you should move farther south to Dunedin. You'd be closer to Middlemarch and other shifters," Sam said. "You'd be closer to the tourist spots. Lots of wealthy people have holiday homes in Queenstown. They're the type who would want security services and yet you'd be able to indulge your feline and wolf more down there. I can introduce my cousin, Saber. He's on the shifter council."

"Thanks. I'll mention it to Henry. Neither of us has seen anything that comes close to what we want. The big earthquakes have caused a strain on the property market and most places are more expensive than our budget."

"Nothing to stop you setting up at Middlemarch. You'd still be close enough to the city."

Gerard nodded, his gaze far-off and thoughtful.

"Sam, I'm leaving," Lisa called.

Sam growled at the sound of the door opening. "Coming," he called and hit the stairs with noisy thumps on his rapid descent.

"What kept you?" Lisa demanded, visibly impatient.

"Saw a biker loitering across the road, and I wanted to watch him to see what he did. Mrs. Humphries and her dog scared him off."

Henry snorted. "She's better than a guard dog."

"She shouldn't be wandering around the neighborhood at this time of the morning," Lisa said in a sharp voice.

"You intend to," Sam said.

"I'm feline and my senses are more highly developed," Lisa retorted. "Are we going or not?"

Sam shared a look with Henry and shrugged. "After you."

Lisa set a brisk pace, desperate to run off the angst—the ball of despair that had settled in the pit of her stomach. This was so damn unfair when she hadn't done a thing wrong. The advertising business was clicky in

Christchurch. She and David used to laugh about the gossip that did the rounds. Not so funny when she was the topic de jour.

Sam must have sensed her need for hard exercise, and he kept up with her pace. She attacked the long incline, the quiet morning soothing the rough edges of her temper. She didn't understand what she'd done wrong, who she'd ticked off enough that they wanted to attack her in this manner. Attack her. Huh! More like destroy her and assassinate her character and good reputation at the same time. She sprinted to the top of the hill and turned right, intending to head to the park as was her normal routine.

Without warning, Sam grabbed her arm and swung her to a halt.

Her temper roared like an angry beast and she fought him off, her breasts heaving from exertion. "Stop manhandling me."

"I told you about the biker. He's parked halfway down that road." Sam shook her and gradually the red film of anger cleared enough for her to hear his patient words.

"What?"

"The biker parked down there looks like the same one who was speaking on his phone outside your house. Have you seen him before?"

"No." She glanced at the bike and frowned. "Now you mention it, I did see a guy on a bike the other morning when I ran. Let's keep running my normal route and see what he does."

"And if he has a gun? Running toward him is plain stupid. We'll run in the opposite direction and look for him again."

"Whatever." Lisa huffed out a breath, aware she sounded like a sulky child. "Sorry. You're right. Let's go. I need to run."

Sam let her set the pace, and she ceased her mad sprint to a speed more resembling a fast jog. This time she cast out her senses and cataloged the morning sounds. A dog barking. The cry of a grumpy baby. A plane rumbled overhead. The faint rustle of the wind in the trees and the swirl of autumn leaves along the ground. Gradually, the traffic sounds increased with workers leaving on their morning commute to jobs in the city.

"If we run up this road, it leads into the one where we saw the bike."

"All right." Sam kept running at her side, his breathing scarcely elevated while hers rasped in and out of her mouth.

They ran silently for the five minutes it took to reach the road.

"He's gone," Sam said.

"Maybe it was a coincidence."

"Could be. It's best to use caution."

"You're right. Thanks for running with me."

"I enjoy spending time with you."

"Even if I'm grumpy?"

"Even then," he said and his voice held humor.

She slowed her pace, going into a warm-down speed. It took another ten minutes before they ran up her driveway and approached the house. She started to do her normal stretches but Sam urged her inside.

"It's safer to be inside."

Lisa opened her mouth to argue, then sighed. "You're right. This situation is making me argumentative."

"I'd say stroppy," Sam offered, the corners of his sexy mouth tilting upward. "I enjoy seeing your different facets."

Lisa huffed out a strangled breath. "It will be worse by the end of the day. I'm cringing at the thought of the fall-out from last night."

"It mightn't be as bad as what you think."

It was worse, much worse than even her imagination could conjure.

Lisa started at the top of her client list, ringing each client and laying out the facts. She'd been accused of copying someone else's design. No, she couldn't prove conclusively that she hadn't used another designer's work.

"So what you're saying is that I need to accept your word against that of the entire Design Award people?" the first client asked.

"I don't know where they obtained their information or who has accused me. All I can say is that the design was my own work, inspired by a walk along the beach."

"I want a refund," the client said in a hostile voice. "I'll take my business elsewhere."

Lisa endeavored to keep her tone even and non-combative. She blinked rapidly. "I'll refund your deposit today." Too bad she'd spent hours on his campaign and he possessed the mock-ups of the final campaign.

Three hours later, she had two clients left and the press release put out by the Design Award committee had stopped any prospective clients from thinking about using her services.

She sat at her desk, her head in her hands and tears pricking at her eyes.

A knock at her office door had her straightening.

Henry stood in the doorway with a coffee mug in one hand and a plate of sandwiches in the other.

"Not hungry."

"You need to eat. Don't let whoever did this win." Henry set the mug and plate on her desk.

"I've lost most of my clients. Some of them have been with me for three years, yet they refuse to believe me. Some of the campaigns are almost finished, but they don't want to associate their companies with me." She let out a snort. "I bet they'll use my work in some form anyway."

"Do the same thing they've accused you of?"

"They won't see it that way. They'll think I used their input, which means the idea belongs to them. No matter what I do I can't win."

"What do you intend to do?"

Her chin lifted. "Not give up. I guess that means I'll have to start with a new name. Maybe try something slightly different for a while. I had one client who is an author. I know she uses American cover artists. There is no reason I couldn't design some covers and set up shop."

"If you ever get tired of Sam—"

"You trying to steal Sam's girl again?" Gerard asked from the doorway.

"Yep," Henry said with an unapologetic grin. "I admire her courage and her inner steel. Most women would be bawling by now."

"Oh, I want to do that," Lisa said.

"Research your cover idea," Henry ordered.

"I need to do the refund payments for my clients," she said. "That's going to clean out my bank account, but I might have some images that would work."

"Can't you use your own photos?"

"I don't have any male—" She broke off to eye both Henry and Gerard. "Would you model for me? I could use you on covers."

"Us?" Gerard asked.

Henry's mouth dropped open and she grinned.

"If you didn't want your faces showing, I could work around that. Would you do it? I'd want bare chests and muscles."

Gerard and Henry shared a glance.

"Check with Sam first," Henry ordered.

Lisa started to object then saw the sense of the suggestion. The last thing she needed was a jealous feline to add to the mix of her topsy-turvy life. "I'll call him."

Chapter 8

Expulsion

Christchurch city center, Advertising Committee office, late afternoon.

An elderly receptionist with steel-gray hair worn in a sleek bob and pale pink lipstick answered her phone and glanced over the top of her glasses at Lisa. "Ms. Jordan, the committee will see you now."

Lisa wiped her sweaty palms down her navy-blue trousers as she stood and picked up her black leather briefcase. She'd gathered every piece of proof she could find to help her case. She'd backed up her preliminary designs and notes from her client meetings on the cloud.

Hopefully, that would be enough. The client contract and final sign-off had been on her hacked computer.

"This way please." The receptionist trotted down a hallway, her sensible heels clip-clopping on the wooden floor. She paused at the last door and tapped with the back of her knuckles.

The door flew open and James stood in the doorway.

Every muscle in Lisa's body went rigid. "James. I didn't realize you were on the committee." Her voice rose toward the end of her sentence until she sounded like a squeaky talking mouse.

"The committee is ready for you," he said, his tone impersonal as he held the door open.

Right. The pariah. Lisa lifted her chin and sailed through the doorway. She scanned the room, the faces of her accusers and came to a halt when she realized the committee members occupied all the chairs, except one. James took possession of the empty chair. Nonplussed, Lisa hovered inside the door, her right hand clutching the handle of her briefcase.

"Ms. Jordan." The elderly man seated at the head of the table cleaned the lenses of his black-rimmed glasses and pushed them up his nose. His gaze didn't meet hers, but fixated on a point beyond her shoulder. "We have summoned you here to officially strike you off the roster of advertising professionals. You are no longer entitled to attend any of our meetings or business functions, to use our association in any way to entice prospective clients, nor will we consider your work for our annual awards. Your behavior is inexcusable, and we cannot condone this sort of conduct from any of our members."

"But—"

"Your annual fees are not refundable," the man declared.

Lisa spoke before he could continue. "I didn't do anything wrong." She attempted to open her briefcase while juggling it with her knees. "I have proof that I—"

"We have seen all the proof we require. You may go now. Right." He picked up a silver pen and tapped on his memo pad. "What is next on the agenda?"

Lisa ceased trying to open her briefcase, her head hanging as she realized that no matter what she said or offered in the way of evidence to clear her name, they didn't intend to listen. Her nostrils flared, and she drew in a sharp breath, a growl rushing up her throat. She barely managed to block the feral sound of her anger from escaping. With another deep breath, she straightened, and she caught a hint of the same scent she'd smelled in her room. The intruder's scent.

Her right hand gripped her briefcase handle and her feline pushed for release, pushing, pushing, pushing against her control until she trembled with both agitation and rage. She scanned the faces of the nine people sitting around the oval table. The sole person she knew was James. He couldn't be her intruder because she'd been on a date with him at the time.

So, one of the others.

She didn't know their names, but it would be easy enough to discover them on the web.

A starting point to discover which one of these people felt threatened enough by her that they'd invaded her home and stolen her peace of mind.

"They'd already made up their minds," Lisa said on arriving back at her house and finding all three men waiting for her. "They had no intention of giving me a fair hearing." She dropped her briefcase by the front door and stomped toward the kitchen. She pulled a bottle of wine from the fridge and sloshed the white Sauvignon Blanc into a glass. "I didn't even have a chance to show them the stuff I'd collected to clear my name. And do you know the worse thing?"

"What?" Sam asked.

"I caught a trace of the intruder's scent in the boardroom. The same scent I smelled all over my house, but they shoved me from the room, and I couldn't pinpoint the source."

"Names," Henry said in a sharp voice, his hip cocked against the kitchen counter.

All three men held beers, and Sam had something meaty cooking in the oven.

"I'm not sure of all of their names, but they should be on the advertising website." While Henry pulled out his phone and started tapping keys, she said, "James Silcock is the only one I can take off the list of suspects. He might be on the committee but he couldn't have done it since he was with me in the restaurant."

Gerard took a sip of his beer. "Henry and I can check them out for you tomorrow. We'll know the right one because we both caught the scent."

"Thanks," Lisa said.

Sam crossed the distance between them and wrapped his arm around her tense shoulders. "I'm sorry."

"Don't be," she said. "I was thinking about alternatives during the drive home. I thought cover design would be something I could do until I cleared my name. But I need to chase this idea for all it is worth. I might not make much, but if I have to get a job waitressing or washing dishes, I can do that. I've done it before. It's the design part I love most. As long as I can do that, I-I think it will be all right."

"Sweetheart, anything I can help with, you just let me know." Sam pressed a kiss to her temple and her stomach did a slow, rolling swoop.

"Pity Henry and Gerard are here," she whispered.

"Hey, I heard that." Gerard shot her a mock glare.

Thursday, the next week

After spending a day photographing Gerard, Henry and Sam in all manner of poses and costumes, Lisa worked on completing her new website. While she used Henry's laptop, Henry worked on clearing hers of the virus. Each night one or all of the three men stayed at the house. Keeping busy helped but each passing day, each pointed snub from people she used to consider colleagues and friends and the loss of one of her last two clients fueled her anger with whomever had instigated her downfall.

Although they'd gathered a list of the committee, contacting each of the members and sniffing them wasn't proving easy. At least four of the committee had left for a conference in Sydney, Australia.

"I guess I should get going," Sam said. "I wish you'd move out to the farm with me."

"I'm not getting pushed out of my home by a creepy stalker." Lisa balled her hands to fists and bit back a snappish reply since this wasn't the first time he'd made the proposal. "I haven't received any communications since before the awards dinner. Maybe that was his big finale or maybe he feels sorry for me because I've lost my business and reputation."

"Or maybe he's just taking a break," Sam said. "You need to take care."

"I'm spending the weekend with you. I'll come out tomorrow as planned."

His expression softened and he brushed his fingers across her cheek. "I like sleeping with you."

"You like sex," she retorted, some of her ire fading at the lusty glow in his green eyes. At least something in her life was working right.

"That too," he agreed with a satisfied and very smug masculine smirk. "I miss you."

Everything inside her softened. "I miss you too. Thank you for agreeing to pose for my covers. Do you think Casey will pose for me?"

"Give her a call and ask."

"I will. I'd like some wolf and leopard shots. Do you think that would be all right?"

"If Henry and Gerard agree."

"I'll ask them. I wanted to take some scenery shots. The preparation has been fun and given me something else to focus on instead of my business train wreck. I need to finish the website, set up a newsletter and I thought I'd attract initial interest by doing a contest for authors. Then I need to do Facebook posts. So much to do." She couldn't believe that with minimal expense she'd managed to do so much already. She planned on doing six paranormal covers plus running a special on some graphics to start with. She refused to let this setback get her down.

"I'll see you tomorrow afternoon, sweetheart." His kiss was hard and passionate and left her gasping for breath, her pulse racing.

"Wow," she said once he'd lifted his head.

"I wouldn't want you to forget me."

"No chance of that."

"I've got another buyer coming for Jessie. Cross your fingers for me."

"A nice buyer?"

"He has a good reputation."

"As long as he doesn't try to kiss you," Lisa said.

"Who is trying to kiss Sam?" Gerard asked. "You going, bro?"

"Yeah, I need to put Jessie through her paces before the buyer arrives tomorrow. Look after Lisa for me."

"Hey." She clicked her fingers in front of Sam's nose. "Right here. Not helpless."

Henry appeared behind Gerard. "We'll watch out for stalkers."

Lisa walked Sam out to his SUV.

"Take care, sweetheart."

"I will. I'm not helpless."

"I know you're not, but my gut is uneasy. Don't go anywhere alone. If you need to go out, please take either Gerard or Henry. Promise."

"I promise." She leaned through the open window and kissed him, then stepped away from the SUV. "Tomorrow. We'll celebrate your sale."

The next morning

Lisa considered going for a run, then recalled her promise to Sam. She ambled over to her bedroom window and peered out at the front of her section and a portion of Mrs. Humphries's house. A moving shadow claimed her attention, and she froze, her breathing easing out when it didn't move again. Imagination. This situation had turned her into a scaredy-cat. She stared at the spot for an instant longer, and when nothing else attracted her attention, she moved to another window and stared out at the road. A vehicle crawled past and a newspaper struck her driveway.

Right, that settled it. Coffee and the morning paper.

Lisa pulled on a pair of black leggings and a long T-shirt. Halfway from her bedroom, she realized she had two male guests, and she retraced her steps to put on underwear.

"Coffee is ready," Gerard called from the kitchen as she tromped down the stairs.

"I'm grabbing the newspaper."

"Be careful."

She didn't need his reminder and would tell him so as soon as she'd taken her first sip of coffee. She unlocked the door and pulled it open, pausing to scent the air before she stepped outside.

A dew-covered pale pink rose sat on her doormat, an envelope sitting beneath the perfect bloom.

Lisa muttered a rude word and sniffed the air. With fingertips in the corner of envelope, she lifted it close enough for her to sniff. Not Sam. Not her intruder. A different scent emanated from the envelope. It smelled more exotic and... Ylang-ylang. That was the scent.

She carted the rose and card back into the house.

"I think my stalker is at it again," she said to Gerard.

"What have you got?"

"A rose and a card."

"Let me see," Henry said. "I have a pair of gloves."

Lisa handed it over without an argument, needing coffee more than she wanted to know about the note.

"*A rose for a beautiful rose*," Henry read.

Gerard rolled his eyes. "He has an original way with words."

"Maybe it's not the stalker. Maybe Sam—"

"If that is the extent of Sam's romantic game, you should run away with me today," Gerard said. "I don't hold much hope for your happy future."

"There's more," Henry said. "There is a verse about comparing Lisa to a summer rose."

"Ah, one of the romantic poets." Gerard wandered over to the coffeepot to top up his mug. "That makes everything all right then."

The doorbell went and they shared glances with one another, uneasy on her part.

"I'll get it," Gerard offered. "The weirdo could still be out there."

Henry scowled at his wristwatch. "It's too early to ring our contact at the police." He produced a plastic bag and placed the card inside. "What do you want to do with the flower?"

"Bin it," she said.

Gerard came back holding a gift basket. "Expecting this?"

"No. Is there a card?"

"Yeah, it's stapled to the side of the basket." Henry retrieved it and opened it with his gloved hands. "Different handwriting. Different-colored pen. Just says enjoy the special treats."

"Same scent as the card with the flower," Gerard said. "Did you see anyone when you were outside?"

"No. I looked but it is still fairly dark."

Henry grunted. "Pity we can't eat some of this stuff. No telling if it's doctored or not."

The doorbell rang again and they all looked at each other again.

"Give me five to sneak around the back," Henry said. "You stay in the house, Lisa."

The doorbell buzzed with impatience this time, the visitor holding it down for long seconds. Henry disappeared while Gerard waited.

"Was anyone at the door when you found the basket?"

"No," Gerard said.

"I didn't sense anyone either."

Lisa sipped her coffee and frowned when the doorbell sliced through the early morning quiet yet again. "Persistent."

Gerard strolled toward her front door.

"Be careful," she called after him. The hairs at the back of her neck prickled as a sense of foreboding swept through her. The coffee she'd swallowed sat uneasily. "He could have a gun."

Outside, a short, sharp yip sounded.

"Henry." Gerard opened the door without hesitation. "Nothing dangerous."

"A bunch of balloons," Lisa said shortly after they sent the deliveryman on his way. "Why?"

Gerard shrugged. "I don't know. There is a note."

"The scent is different." She opened the pale pink envelope, which matched the red, white and pink balloons. "From my secret admirer." She glanced up at Gerard and Henry, who had remained in wolf form. "I could do without a secret admirer."

"That's all it says?" Gerard asked.

"Yes. Anyone fancy scrambled eggs and bacon?"

Henry gave an affirmative growl, so she made herself busy in the kitchen.

"If Sam decides he doesn't want you, you'll hook up with me," Gerard declared as he leaned back with a satisfied sigh.

Henry grinned. "Not if I fight you for the right. A beautiful shifter and a good cook. What do you say?"

Lisa shook her head at their silliness. "Since I cooked, the pair of you can do the dishes. I want to tweak my website and go live with my new business."

Two hours passed before she was satisfied with her website and the contest to introduce herself to prospective customers.

Henry tapped on her office door. "Your computer is clear of viruses now. I've added extra layers of security for you. Would you like me to show you?"

"Please."

Henry took her through the new programs and security, plus he insisted on new passwords and an identity safe.

"That is brilliant. Thanks so much, Henry."

"All part of the service and a thanks for letting us stay here while we research locations for our business."

"Sam said he suggested Dunedin. Do you think you might go farther south?"

"It's looking that way. There are advantages of living closer to the Middlemarch shifter community. Gerard has gone to check another vacant building, but the rent is on the high side."

The doorbell rang.

Lisa sighed. "I thought the deliveries had stopped."

"I'll get it."

"No, it might be Mrs. Humphries. I bet she's wondering what all the fuss is about."

Henry tugged off his T-shirt. "I'll shift and be at your side, just in case."

Lisa rolled her eyes but didn't argue. The doorbell went yet again and she increased her pace. As she opened the door, she heard the click of claws on her wooden floors.

It wasn't Mrs. Humphries.

It was a policeman.

"Yes." Her gaze went to the plain sedan parked in her driveway. "Can I help you?"

"Are you Lisa Jordan?"

"Yes. Can I help you, Officer?" The vibe from this guy raised her hackles but she couldn't work out why. Beside her, Henry growled in a low rumble.

His tanned face broke into a broad grin. "My lucky day."

"Pardon?"

He bent over and clicked a button on a boom box she hadn't noticed. Loud music with a raunchy beat burst in vibrant life. He stepped back, his grin remaining toothy.

"No," Lisa said in a faint voice, and she edged inside a fraction.

Henry made a weird chuffing noise—wolfish humor—while Lisa gaped at the dancing cop. He twirled and gyrated, then whipped off his shirt to display a hairless chest that glowed even under the weak sunshine. His hips rocked, his pelvis made a circle, drawing her unwilling gaze. He did four rapid thrusts.

"It's definitely a male," she muttered.

Henry chuffed again, leaning his weight against her leg.

Mrs. Humphries appeared in her front door, and even from where she stood, Lisa could see her wide eyes. A particularly loud blast of music drew her attention back to the cop. He sauntered closer, took off his hat and placed it on Lisa's head, then he drew her into some moves that resembled dirty dancing.

Lisa opened her mouth to protest and attempted to pull away but the stripper cop held her tight. He stole a kiss and freed her, doing several impressive hip grinds to the beat of the music. His hands wandered to the band of his low-rise trousers and with one hard jerk, the black fabric split and fell away from his impressive body.

Lisa felt her mouth drop open as she stared at his briefs. He waggled his butt, and she saw Mrs. Humphries clap her hand over her mouth.

"Ah," Lisa said and took half a step backward.

The stripper cop spun and waggled his bare butt cheeks in her direction.

The man wore a G-string.

Lisa backed up again, but Henry darted behind her, blocking a retreat.

"Move," she ordered.

He made that weird chuffing sound.

"I'll tell Sam you made me watch."

The stripper shook his groove thing in her direction as the music trailed to an end.

"Get it off," Mrs. Humphries shouted. "*Whoop! Whoop!*" Geoffrey, her dog, barked three times.

The music cut off and Lisa froze.

At least he'd kept his G-string. As the thought formed, his hands went to the G-string and he whipped it free of his body.

"Turn around!" Mrs. Humphries hollered.

Lisa, after one quick glance, raised her gaze and kept it on the man's face. "Who are you and why are you here?"

"Your secret admirer thought you might enjoy the entertainment," the stripper said. He didn't seem to have a problem with standing naked at her front door.

A car slowed and the driver honked his horn. Mrs. Humphries cheered and Henry made his chuffing sound of amusement.

"Who booked your services?"

"No idea. Doesn't matter. Did you enjoy my performance? I haven't been working for this company for long. I'd love to know what you thought."

"Um, very interesting," Lisa said. "Is that all? You seem to be causing a traffic jam on my street."

"One more thing," the stripper said. "I'm meant to give you this." He handed over a white envelope. "Thanks for being such a sexy audience."

"Um, yeah," Lisa said. "Why don't you take your bow at my neighbor's house? She seemed to enjoy your performance. Um..." What did one say to a stripper? "Thank you."

This time Henry allowed her to retreat and she stepped inside, closing her front door.

Henry shifted and stalked to the kitchen in front of her to where he'd left his clothes. She was so rattled, she didn't even take the time to sneak a peek at his muscular backside.

Chapter 9

Neighbors and Red Ribbons

"Well, that was interesting." Lisa plonked herself on a chair at the table in her kitchen. She scarcely blinked when Henry pulled on a pair of faded jeans to screen his nakedness.

"What kind of man wears a red ribbon around his dick?" Henry demanded. "I don't know whether to scrub my eyeballs or snigger."

For a long instant, they stared at each other, then Lisa broke out laughing. "I wish I'd had a camera."

"I hope they paid him well. What does the card say?"

"Should I use gloves?"

Henry handed her the pair he'd used. "Might as well."

Lisa donned them and opened the envelope. Several photos fell from the card inside. She gasped. "He *has* been following me. I've sensed him but never caught him or saw a thing out of place. That's me at the supermarket. And at the office supplies shop. Filling up my car with petrol." Then there was the other photos of her running with Sam, of her in the garden with Henry and in the driveway with Gerard. Some of the photos showed her laughing with the men, their arms wrapped around her. She and Sam kissing.

"Lay the photos out on the table," Henry ordered.

She did as he instructed, and they stared at them. In each of the photos where she appeared with Sam, Henry or Gerard, someone had scrubbed out their faces with a red marker pen.

"None of them are taken at Sam's farm. They're all around your section or in the city."

"I'll ring the police and let them know of the morning's activities, get those to them," Henry said. "I think you should stay with Sam."

She nodded, a sick sensation settling in her gut. "Why? What have I done to this person? Sam might ring or text or send me flowers, but he'd never send a stripper. He'd be more likely to—"

Henry held up his right hand in a stop signal. "I don't want to hear that one of my best friends wears a ribbon around his dick."

The sound of a key sounded in the door, and they both stiffened.

"Wait here. I'll make sure it's Gerard."

Lisa didn't even bother arguing, which told her the morning's events had shaken her more than she'd admitted.

"Hey, what's with the gun?" Gerard asked.

"A precaution. We've had a busy morning," she heard Henry answer.

"You all right, Lisa?" Gerard burst into the kitchen, his expression fierce. "Do you want us to ring Sam?"

"No. I'll finish my work here and go out later this afternoon as planned."

"Crap, he's escalating." Gerard dropped into the chair opposite her and scanned the photos.

"You missed the stripper," she said.

"He wore a red bow around his dick," Henry added with a chortle.

"You're shittin' me," Gerard said.

Lisa shook her head. "You ask Mrs. Humphries. She might have missed the bow, but she saw the rest from her front door.

The doorbell peeled.

"I'll go," Gerard said.

He returned minutes later with Mrs. Humphries and her terrier. Geoffrey growled at Gerard, did his usual teeth-snapping at Lisa and circled them both to sidle up to Henry. Henry, he licked.

"Well," Mrs. Humphries said. Her gaze lingered on Henry's bare chest. "Things are very strange around here today. I thought your birthday was in December, dear. What are those?"

Nothing wrong with her eyesight, Lisa thought, as Gerard moved to block her view of the photos.

"What's going on? Do you have a stalker? Are you two the police?"

Nothing wrong with her brain either.

"Henry and Gerard are friends," Lisa said in a firm voice.

"But you have a stalker."

Lisa sighed. "Yes."

"I knew something strange was going on," Mrs. Humphries said. "I've noticed you're never alone now. And you're much slower to answer the door. I saw the man with the motorbike deliver the rose this morning."

"What time? Did you see his face?" Henry demanded.

"No, it was still dark. He picked the flower from my neighbor's garden then walked past my house and up your driveway. I don't sleep as much as I used to and happened to be looking out the window at the time."

"Have you seen him before?" Henry asked.

She cocked her head and her eyelashes fluttered at Henry. Lisa swallowed a laugh. It seemed both dog and master had fallen for Henry.

"I've seen the bike a few times. The man spends a lot of time on his phone, but I've never seen his face and he doesn't live in our street. He wears his helmet and it screens a great deal of his face. Should I watch for him?"

"No," Henry said in a sharp voice. "He could be dangerous. I'll contact the police and mention you've seen him loitering."

"An old boyfriend, dear?"

"No," Lisa said.

Mrs. Humphries patted Lisa's hand. "You'll be safe with the three strapping men about the place. Is one of them your boyfriend?"

Gerard bit off a laugh, and Lisa saw a flash of amusement in Henry.

"Yes," Lisa said. "Did you need something Mrs. Humphries?"

A trace of frustration showed in her neighbor's frown then her features cleared. "I've brought you a bag of sugar." She plucked it out of her handbag and placed it on the table. "You're always giving me sugar and I thought it was time I repaid you."

"Thank you, Mrs. Humphries."

When her neighbor continued to linger, Lisa jerked her chin at Henry.

"We have a lot to do, Mrs. Humphries. Shall I escort you home?"

"Oh!" A faint pinkness filled her lined cheeks. "That would be nice, young man."

"Henry," Henry said.

Mrs. Humphries let out a girlish giggle. "That would be lovely, Henry."

Henry grabbed his shirt and pulled it on.

"Don't get dressed on my account," Mrs. Humphries said and giggled again.

Henry kept his expression blank and gestured her to precede him from the kitchen.

"After you, Henry," Mrs. Humphries said.

"She wants to ogle his butt," Lisa whispered to Gerard.

The terrier circled both her and Gerard then stood in the doorway and growled at them before trotting after his master and Henry.

Henry returned a few minutes later. "I need a shower," he said. "Tell me she didn't ogle my arse."

"Okay," Lisa said.

"She didn't undress you in her mind," Gerard said.

Henry groaned. "I'm going to take a shower." He shook his head. "This morning has been plain weird."

Her phone went and she reached for it, answering even as she laughed at Henry.

"Did you like my gifts?"

"Which gifts did you send me?"

Gerard moved closer in order to hear and Henry returned soundlessly to stand on her other side.

"You didn't like my stripper. You seem to be into men. I mean, living with three different men. Do they share you around?"

Gerard took the phone from her limp fingers and hung up. "Did you record? It must be someone you know since he rings your cell phone number."

"I recorded it." She chewed a fingernail. "It wouldn't be difficult to obtain my number. I have it on my business cards."

"You need to make a list of your ex-clients for the police," Gerard said. "Just in case."

"All right."

"What number did he ring from?"

Lisa scanned her last call and recited the number for Gerard to jot down. "Chances are it's a prepay phone."

"Possibly, but some of these people make mistakes."

The phone rang again and Lisa scanned the number. "It's Sam."

"I'll go take that shower," Henry said.

Gerard left with him, giving her some privacy.

"Hi, Sam."

"How has your morning been, sweetheart? I miss you."

Everything inside her went soft then pulled tight. "I've had a crazy morning. I'll tell you later."

"I wish I was there."

Lisa smiled at the husky emotion in his voice. "I wish you were too. I'll be out this afternoon as planned, but if it's all right with you, I might stay a bit longer. My house doesn't feel safe anymore."

"I'm pleased you're staying with me, but I wish the cops would catch this guy."

"At least they'll take it a bit more serious now," Lisa said. "Did the buyer like Jessie?"

"Yes, and he didn't quibble about the price. He wants first option on Jessie's younger brother too."

"That's great! We'll celebrate once I get there."

"We will." He lowered his voice. "I have big plans for our night."

"Sounds great." She glanced down at the photos and shivered on seeing one of her and Sam. Along with the red pen, someone had scraped away Sam's face, leaving just paper. This guy was a fruitcake, and she had no idea of his identity. While good at voices, she hadn't recognized his. "I'll see you in a few hours. Want me to bring anything?"

"All sorted," Sam said. "I picked up some groceries on the way home. Stay safe. I'll see you soon."

Henry walked into the kitchen, freshly showered. "I'll drive you to the police station. I spoke with our contact, and he said to bring everything in with us."

The doorbell went yet again.

"I'll get it," Henry said.

Lisa straightened, a burst of fury driving her to action. "No, this is my house. I will answer the door." She stomped from the kitchen to the entrance hall and flung open the door. "Yes," she snapped.

James Silcock stood before her, clutching a bunch of white and yellow daisies. He took half a step back at her ferocious tone.

Lisa stared at him, shocked and angry anew at his cheek in standing on her doorstep with flowers. "What do you want?"

He extended the flowers and hesitated at her lack of expected reaction. Finally, he dropped his hand to his side, the pollen from the daisies leaving a yellow mark on his black trousers. "I wanted to say I'm sorry. I know you and your work ethics. I know that you'd never steal someone else's design."

Lisa found herself gaping at the man. "But you were at the meeting."

"Pardon?"

"The meeting where the advertising committee accused me of stealing and kicked me out of their precious association."

"But—"

"You were there and accused me of theft."

"Excuse me." He thrust the flowers at her and stalked off before she could get out another word. The tires of his car shrieked as he fishtailed from her driveway.

"He looked shocked," Henry said.

Lisa sighed and picked up the flowers she'd dropped. "One more weird in a day of weird occurrences. I'll give these to Mrs. Humphries. I can see she's busy watching." She paused to wing a smirk in Henry's direction. "Unless you want to deliver them."

"No," Henry said, retreating a step.

"Would that be a hell no?" Lisa asked.

"Yep. I'll get the photos into an evidence bag," Henry said. "Make sure no one is lurking behind that tree."

Sam's Farm, outside Christchurch

Despite a successful day, tension resided in his shoulders and worry clamped his chest tight for the hours until he saw Lisa. Gerard drove and waved at Sam when he approached. He drove away, leaving Lisa, her overnight bag and computer bag standing in the driveway.

"Hi," she said.

Sam kept walking until he closed the distance between them. Seconds later, his mouth covered hers in a hungry kiss.

"Go, boss!" Casey shouted.

Sam's growl vibrated against her lips, but he never lightened up on the kiss, only pulling back when they were both breathless. His feline, previously edgy as him, rumbled out a purr, and Lisa laughed.

She stroked his cheek and smiled. "I've missed you, and we've only been apart a few hours."

"At least you won't need to look over your shoulder while you're here," he said.

"The cops know I'm here, but they said I should be careful. Henry, Gerard and I decided I should leave my car at home. Gerard made sure we weren't followed."

"Why did he leave?"

"He got word of a building that might work for them, and he wanted to take a look before someone snapped it up."

"You look tense, like you need a good run. I want to check the cattle in the far paddock where we've run before. Would you like to do that?"

"Yes." Lisa's features held strain, and he longed to ease some of her worries. "It's been a hell of a day."

"Walk or drive?"

"Walk. It will take me that long to tell you everything that has happened since you last saw me."

"Sounds interesting." His smile faded when she didn't return the sentiment. "That bad?"

"Like all good stories it hits high and low points." Her attempt at levity failed to echo in her beautiful blue eyes.

Sam stepped back and picked up her bag. He reached for her hand with his free one, taking comfort from the physical contact.

Ten minutes later, they strolled along the fence line, on the way to check his herd of cows. He listened while Lisa spoke. The tension he'd felt before her arrival grew again and he had to tamp down his anger. His feline tested his control and his canines pushed past his gums to greater prominence.

Then he focused on what she said next. "A red bow? What sort of man wears a bow around his dick?"

"Exactly what Henry said."

His momentary humor dissipated when she mentioned the photos.

"And both Mrs. Humphries and Geoffrey, her terrier, have a crush on Henry. She fluttered her eyelashes like a champ and Geoffrey did his usual performance with me, growled at Gerard then trotted over to Henry and kept licking him. Love at first sight."

A chuckle burst free. "I would have paid to see that."

"Next time I go home, we'll invite Mrs. Humphries over for a cup of tea. You can watch the Mrs. Humphries and Henry show yourself."

Sam led her to a lone totara tree, its thick girth rough with gnarly bark. "We can shift here. These cows are used to me in feline form but go slow around the calves. Then, I want to check the trough to make sure nothing has upset the water flow."

"I like you in farmer mode."

"I like you in any mode."

Lisa smiled at his words, but it didn't come near the full-out smile he'd come to enjoy. His anger pulsed in him like a heartbeat, his inability to fix the problem eating at him.

"What did the police say?"

"They told me to stay with other people and not to venture out on my own. If they have time, they'll do a drive past my house. Basically, it's the same story. They can't do much unless we discover the culprit's identity."

"Any common scents?"

"No, every card smelled different. Henry started following up with the suppliers but so far, the orders came in via phone or the internet. Oh, I forgot to tell you about James Silcock. He arrived at the house with a bunch of flowers, saying how sorry he was about the accusations circulating about me. And when I confronted him about his behavior at the meeting, he started to speak, thrust the flowers at me and left mid-word. Talk about weird." She shook her head. "Really peculiar."

"I never liked the man."

A spurt of humor danced into her expression and his mood lightened too. "Really? I thought it was because he asked me out on a date."

"He has a weak chin."

Lisa pulled off her jacket and yanked her T-shirt over her head to display a black lacy bra. "I thought it was his species—male and human."

"That too. You're beautiful. I'm lucky I went to the Middlemarch Singles Ball. I almost didn't."

"You have grown into a very sexy man."

Sam let out a feline growl, both man and beast thrilled with her words and the expression in her eyes. She belonged to them, and happiness, the like of which he'd seldom felt before blazed within him, almost too big for his body to hold.

"I want you, but I also want privacy and a soft bed."

She shrugged free of her sexy bra and reached over to squeeze his forearm. "That sounds perfect. We could even share a shower."

"Sold." Sam toed off his boots and dispersed with his clothes. With a glance at Lisa, he stood back and called up his feline. His shift tore through him, muscles and bones reshaping in rapid efficiency, black fur rippling across his bare skin and cutting through the wind pummeling his nakedness.

He waited for Lisa to complete her shift, and unable to help himself, he padded over to her and brushed his head against her shoulder. She gave a rumble of pleasure, and some of the angst riding him shifted. At least he could give her this. Sooner or later, her stalker would make a mistake and the cops would get him. And if they failed to act, he, Henry and Gerard could take care of matters. One way or another, Lisa would be safe.

The exercise, the hot shower, dinner and a few glasses of wine had relaxed her. Lisa mulled over the idea of firing up her laptop to check on her new enterprise. No. Tomorrow would be soon enough.

"I like having you here. Would you consider moving in with me?"

"Selling my house?"

"Yes. I care for you, Lisa. You're my mate, and I know your feline is nudging you in the same direction."

Nothing less than the truth. She'd felt the rightness of being with Sam from the instant she'd seen him at the dance. Sleeping with him had reinforced the feelings, and no matter how much she returned to the age thing, bottom line, her feline wanted him.

"Before I met you and for a while afterward, I used to talk to David in my mind, discuss things when I felt lonely or had a problem. I haven't done that as much recently." She peeked at him to see if he considered her crazy.

"That's natural. You loved David and I accept that you'd still think of him now and then. I wish I'd known him because everything I've heard from Middlemarch tells me he was a good man, a good husband."

Lisa sighed, regret surfacing as it always did when she thought of David. "It was difficult losing him that way, knowing if he were feline, he could have fought the illness better. David told me to give you a chance." She didn't shy away from meeting his gaze this time, and instead of the *you're crazy* look she expected she got curiosity and a quizzical gleam.

"He did?"

"I almost lost it when I saw your female buyer kissing you. He pushed me to see past first impressions."

Sam sobered. "A woman like her would never grab my interest. I don't care if she badmouths me. I've never slept with buyers to get sales, and I'm not about to start that. Besides, there is only one woman who interests me."

"The age thing doesn't bother you, does it? I seesaw back and forth on the matter."

"Felines live longer than humans anyway. We're doing fine together, and I can't see that changing. My feline wants yours as his mate. I want you, and that's all that matters."

"Are you asking me?"

He caressed her cheek and she angled her face into the intimate touch. "Something for you to consider. I've known you're my mate for years."

Lisa felt her mouth drop open, and she snapped it shut. "While I babysat for you and your sisters?"

He nodded. "I knew I had to wait. I was too young and you'd never have considered the possibilities."

"But I married David. What if David hadn't become sick and died?"

"Sometimes there is more than one mate. There was nothing I could do. That's another part of the reason I went to Australia then joined the army."

Sadness wrenched at Lisa and a sense of awe too. Not many felines would display the same maturity. She wasn't certain she could have exercised the same patience and acceptance if she were in his position.

"I'm not telling you this to make you feel guilty. I know you loved David. Your love for your husband has molded you into the person you are now, the woman I want."

"Then why are you telling me?"

"Because I want you to understand my feelings for you aren't casual. They're not a whim, and you won't find me boasting to my friends that I can hook an older woman. I want you to know I'm in this for the long haul."

She opened her mouth to speak and Sam placed his fingers over her lips.

"No more talk. I want to take you to bed and explore this luscious body of yours. We'll discuss this again once you've become used to the idea, and we've got rid of your stalker. Okay?" He removed his hand, the glow in his green eyes mesmerizing and beautiful.

Her pulse rate picked up, surprise and astonishment warring for supremacy. She found herself nodding, and he tugged her to her feet. Without warning, he seized her and slung her over his shoulder. His big hand swatted her jeans-clad butt when she attempted to wriggle.

"Cease," he ordered. "Don't make me drop you."

"I'll bite your butt."

Sam chuckled as he strode from the lounge and down the passage toward his bedroom. "Woman, excellent idea. You go right ahead."

Lisa spluttered out a laugh and pinched his bottom instead.

"I could always spank you for misbehavior."

Lisa stilled while pondering the idea. Heat collected in her face, and it was nothing to do with the way she draped upside down over his shoulder. Surprisingly, she quite liked the idea of spanking.

"Cat got ya tongue," he taunted.

A snort escaped her, and Sam chuckled as he dropped her onto the bed. She immediately bounded to her feet. "I want to undress you."

He looked nonplussed for a second, then shrugged. "Go right ahead."

Lisa dropped to her knees in front of him and tugged off his thick woolen socks one at a time. His hand pressed lightly on her head for balance, and she kept thinking of his earlier words. He'd wanted her as a teenager. The thought should have freaked her out, but instead, admiration filled her. That level of maturity was rare. She unfastened his belt, drew it free from the loops, and set it aside. She thought back to her teenage self—full of self-importance and the world-belongs-to-me attitude—and realized she would have gone after what she wanted, no matter the obstacles, the consequences.

And if she'd been in the same position, nothing would have come of the relationship because of the age difference. Years mattered at that stage of life, but now, not so much.

She opened the button fastening on his jeans and slid down the fly zipper.

"Lisa?"

"Hmmm?"

"I have a limited store of patience." His soft words held a warning and another reminder of the patience he'd exercised to date.

She glanced up at him and winked. "I'll keep that in mind."

Lisa slid her fingers between the denim and his body, savoring the heat and the slight hint of his scent—one of musk and aftershave and arousal. She let her fingers drift downward and felt the swelling of his cock. Good. The heat was affecting him too.

"Lisa."

"Yes, Sam?"

"Clock is ticking."

"Hmmm, I can hear it. It's very loud. Wretched thing kept me awake the last time I spent the night here." She grasped the band of his jeans and yanked them downward, baring his corded thighs. He stepped out of the denim, kicking his jeans aside.

"Have I told you how much I admire your body? Broad shoulders. Your lickable abs. Tight butt." She slipped her fingers behind him and gave him a sly pinch.

He jumped then sent her a reproving look. "You don't need to show your appreciation in that way."

She grinned. "No?"

"I can think of better places for you to touch." His eyes glowed with desire and passion and an indefinable something that made her heart beat just that little bit faster.

"I need a map."

"No, you don't. I'm a guy. Use logic."

She tickled the backs of his knees, ignoring his blooming erection. "I might need a clue."

Sam grunted, and she saw the exact second that impatience got the better of him. He moved with feline-quickness, lifting her off her feet and tossing her onto the bed. She bounced once before his hard, hot body covered hers.

"Not laughing now," he taunted.

"I'm still wearing clothes." No, there was nothing smug about her comeback. Nothing smug at all.

Sam met her gaze—the one that held not a scrap of challenge or satisfaction—and said in a silky voice, "Do you have sentimental attachment to this shirt?"

Lisa glanced downward to take in the blue chambray fabric of her shirt—an older one she'd dragged from the depths of her wardrobe because it was warm, comfortable and perfect for the cooler autumn days. "Why?"

"Because I've taken a dislike to it." And with that, he grasped the neckline and yanked. Fabric ripped and buttons flew. Seconds later, Sam had the remnants of the shirt in his hands and he dropped it over the side of the bed. "You can wear one of mine."

His gaze went to her bra—a navy-blue one this time.

"Don't you dare."

"Is that a challenge?"

"Let me up so I can strip."

"As long as you don't decide to get huffy."

Lisa snorted. "I started this. Actions have consequences."

His glance held surprise, then appreciation. "I like you. A lot. I'll help with the undressing."

It wasn't a question or a request.

Lisa paused, testing inwardly as to how she felt about orders. A sizzle of heat crawled through her veins, warming her body as it slid downward to gather in a ball of lust between her thighs. Okie dokie then.

On trembling legs, she stood quietly and waited for Sam. His eyes glowed with feline alpha satisfaction and when his lips tipped up into a smile, she noted his prominent canines.

He stalked a circle around her, and she started at the touch of his hand on her right shoulder.

"Your pretty bra first. I do enjoy your lingerie."

Already noted and exploited to the fullest. She bit back a grin at the thought and realized how comfortable she felt with Sam. Her inner voices or ghost, whichever came nearest the truth, seemed to agree because David hadn't offered an opinion.

Competent hands flicked the hook closure of her bra and her breasts spilled free. A wave of desire gripped her as his callused fingers slid the silky fabric down her arms. He tossed that on the floor too.

"Jeans." Competent fingers worked the fastenings and slid the denim down her legs. Her thick socks came away at the same time. He stood back to study her as she stood in the navy-blue bikini briefs. "Pretty."

He stalked her and she backed up toward the bed. "Oh, no. Don't you dare rip them."

"Better take them off quick," he whispered, pouncing before she had time to get out a squeak.

But before she could wriggle free of the last of her clothing, he whisked them down her legs.

"Much better," he said. "Hands under your head. Don't move them until I say you can. Show me your pussy."

She blinked, considered, then shifted her position to the middle of the bed and followed his orders. A hard, satisfied purr rippled through her mind while every particle in her body sat up and took notice of Sam.

"You're beautiful, Lisa." He settled in the V between her legs and brushed a kiss to her inner thigh. He took a deep breath, dragging in her scent then lifted his head to give her a slow, sexy smile of satisfaction. "You want me."

"Goes without saying."

"I can see your feline in your eyes."

"I can see yours," she countered.

He slid his mouth up her thigh toward the heart of her. "It's never been like this for me before."

185

Her neither. The quick glance they exchanged propelled her to give him the words. He deserved nothing less. "I loved David, but being with him was different. You're feline and sex with you is the best I've ever had. There is the pleasure, but there is an inner satisfaction that makes everything better."

He didn't say anything, but something clicked, the last vestiges of inner restraint broke and she experienced a new lightness. He swiped his tongue along her cleft, rougher than normal. Every nerve ending saluted, and she groaned when he stopped short of her clit.

A huff of warm air against her flesh told of his amusement, but since he licked another sensual path across her sex, she relaxed and settled back to enjoy the torture.

"You taste good," he whispered. "I can't get enough of you. When you're not with me, I miss you and wonder what you're doing. I think of you throughout the day. And when you're with me, I want to crawl into your body and never leave."

A surprised giggle burst free. "That might scare your buyers."

He licked her a third time, giving her clit a light flick. "It might at that." He pushed a finger past her entrance, her body ready for his possession. His lips settled over her swollen clit and teased the nub until tiny darts of pleasure assailed her. He stroked his finger into her with easy slides and stretched her by adding another one to the mix.

Lisa groaned and lifted her hips in an attempt to ride the enjoyable sensations beginning to course through her body.

He lifted his head, her clit giving a throb of protest at the loss of contact. "Keep still."

"But—"

"Still or I stop."

"Meanie."

"Sweetheart, my feline is on edge. Please don't push me now." His tone had her staring, her mind busily working, and she couldn't make up her mind as to what he meant. She ended up nodding her assent even as she puzzled as to his meaning. She could ask. If he meant a mating and marking— Her breath caught. Something to think about later when her emotions weren't clamoring for climax.

He resumed his licks, his teasing caresses, coaxing then shoving her into a fiery passion that stole her breath and had her calling out his name.

"Sam." She shuddered and twitched. Somewhere along the line, she'd disobeyed and moved her hands. Now, her fingers gripped his hair with each jerk of her hips.

He continued his lazy licks until her tremors subsided and gave a satisfied smile when he lifted his head. "I enjoyed that."

"Me too."

"Good." He moved, shifting his body over hers until they were face-to-face. His kiss was unhurried, a sweet seduction of her tangled senses. She tasted herself on his lips, felt the abrasiveness of his tongue and used her own to lash one of his canines. He groaned against her mouth, shifting positions and fitting his cock to her entrance. He slid inside her, going much slower than she'd assumed he would.

Each stroke caught a sweet spot deep inside her, and she lifted into his thrusts, greedily striving for another orgasm.

"Touch yourself," he whispered against her lips. "Won't last much longer."

Lisa hesitated, then thought why not. It might be greedy wanting more—no craving more—but that still didn't make it wrong. She squeezed her hand between their straining bodies, giving herself that bit of extra stimulation.

"I like feeling your hand."

Surprised, she glanced at him, saw he'd advanced into his shift. The thrust of his cock felt bigger, his width filling her to capacity.

"That's what you do to me," he whispered.

Lisa allowed her stroking finger to travel a fraction farther, so she massaged her clit and the base of his cock with each sweeping move.

Sam groaned. His big frame trembled, and she felt the rapid and convulsive heave of his shaft as he came.

Close. So close.

She moved her finger and clung to him, riding each of his rapid thrusts. On the last thrust before he stilled, pleasure bloomed in her—softer and less encompassing than the previous orgasm—but enjoyable nonetheless.

Chests heaving, they clung to one another, enjoying the rush of blood and the closeness of their bodies.

Sam was right. This was the best sex she'd ever had.

Chapter 10

Stalkers and Research

H er cell phone rang the next morning while they were having breakfast. She checked the number before answering. "It's Henry. Hi, Henry."

"Someone tried to break into your house early this morning. Gerard met some bird, but I wasn't feeling the party mood and left around one. Bastard must've heard my car pull into the driveway. I heard a bike start up, and by the time I realized, he had gone."

"So he didn't get inside?"

Sam shot her a sharp glance of inquiry and moved closer in order to hear.

"No, the new locks on the ground floor proved more difficult than your old ones."

"Good. Thank goodness I listened to you about renewing more of the window locks. Did you report it to the cops?"

"My next job after I finish talking to you. I'll check with Mrs. Humphries, but I doubt she would've seen anything at that time of the morning. There was no moon."

Lisa frowned. "What about his scent? Anything familiar?"

"Smell says the same guy who broke in the first time. Same citrus scent."

"The cops promised they'd do some drive-bys," Lisa said.

"I've seen a plain car once and Gerard said he saw a cop car around five yesterday afternoon."

Anger bloomed in her. This wasn't right, and she hated the fact she needed to move out of her own home because of this idiot. "This is bullshit," she said. "The cops are powerless to act until we learn his identity. We're shifters. I say we set a trap for the coward and teach him a lesson he won't forget."

"No," Sam said.

"She's right," Henry said at the same time.

"Sam, we could do this between us. Our senses are much better."

"What if he has a gun or another type of weapon?" Sam countered.

"We have the element of surprise," Lisa said. "He won't expect big black leopards or a wolf. In the moment when he's wondering if he's seeing things, we'll have him."

"Then what?" Sam asked.

"Lisa can ring the cops and say she caught a man on her property and she thinks he's her stalker."

"And if he tells the police about us?" Sam asked.

"Who is going to believe him?" Lisa scoffed.

"We could spill alcohol on him," Henry said. "They might think he's been drinking."

"Sam, I can't keep living this way. I need to be able to do my morning run or go to my mailbox without worrying about a weirdo attempting to grab me."

Sam sighed, and she knew she'd convinced him.

"I'll drive Lisa in this afternoon and we can work out a plan," he said.

"See you then," Henry said and hung up.

Sam's expression held concern, and she wrapped her arm around his waist and pressed her face against his chest. "I'm not taking this lightly. Between the four of us we can work out a plan to end this harassment."

Sam cursed and scratched the back of his neck. "I know you're right, and this is the logical step, but that doesn't mean I have to like the plan."

"What chores do you have today? Do you have time to spend in town to help me?"

"I'll make time," Sam said. "Because I'm sure as hell not letting you place yourself in danger without me being there to guard your back."

The house on Beechwood Drive didn't feel like home any longer. She climbed from the passenger seat of Sam's SUV and scanned the grounds, searching for anything or anyone out of place.

Henry opened the front door and came out to meet them with Gerard on his heels.

"Any luck with the building?" Lisa asked.

Gerard grinned. "You trying to get rid of us?"

"No, but if you're heading south, I'll give you my sister's name or Sam will let his cousins know you're heading in. They might know of suitable premises."

Henry slid his arm around her waist and ignored Sam's grumble of complaint. "We're not leaving until we catch your stalker."

Lisa kissed Henry's cheek, also ignoring Sam's grumbling. "Thank you. Did you see Mrs. Humphries?"

"She went out for the day. Took the dog with her. What is its name anyway?"

Lisa grinned. "Geoffrey."

Henry barked out a laugh. "Very dignified."

"I've made coffee," Gerard said. "We need to discuss our plan."

"We all know there is one plan that will work," Sam said as they moved into the kitchen and took seats around the kitchen table.

"Which is?" Henry asked.

"You guys need to make yourself scarce and leave me alone in the house tonight," Lisa answered and kept her voice even despite the tremors in the pit of her stomach. "You need to make a production of leaving and sneak back once it's dark."

The doorbell rang, and Lisa stood. "I'll get it."

Sam started to protest, but she held up her hand in a stop motion.

"No, let me do this. This stalker—this man—has made me feel unsafe in my own home. I need to start reclaiming my rights, and that means answering my front door."

"Lisa, be—"

"Sam, she's right. Let her have her independence," Henry said.

Lisa sucked in a quick breath and reached for the doorknob. Her hand displayed a distinct tremor, and she snatched it back and wiped her palm down her jeans.

Forcing herself to calmness, she inhaled and pushed out the breath of air. Then, she allowed her feline senses full rein. Nothing shouted an alarm, so she pulled open the door.

A pimple-faced youth with carrot-red hair stood on her doorstep, his right hand clutching a bouquet of balloons. A myriad of colors, they jostled each other in the breeze. "Miss Jordan?"

"Yes."

"These are for you." He handed them over and produced a white envelope. "This goes with the balloons. Sign here please."

Lisa thrust the balloons inside and released the strings. The helium balloons darted to the ceiling and trapped by the flat surface, jostled for space. The youth's scent wasn't familiar. "Who sent them?"

The youth pushed a piece of gum into his mouth and commenced chewing. "No idea. I just deliver."

Lisa signed for the balloons and after scanning the street for vehicles, backed into the house. She left the balloons in the foyer and strode into her kitchen with the card. Sam, who had been pacing, spun to face her, clear relief in his expression.

"It was a delivery man with a bunch of balloons. This is the card." She wanted to thrust it at one of the men and tell them to open it, but she quelled the instinct. Instead, she ripped open the envelope. Several photos dropped out, along with a sheet of paper. Lisa forced herself to study them. "They're recent photos. Crap. This one is in my bedroom." She shunted the offending photo across the surface of her wooden table. "I don't usually close my blinds because no one overlooks my bedroom. He would have needed to climb into the totara tree in my garden to take this photo." The photo showed her in her bra and panties, and she was glad she didn't habitually wander through her bedroom naked.

"I'll hand these on to our cop contact. Even if we decide to take action on our own we need to keep up the chain of evidence," Henry said.

"Sam, how about a romantic stroll around my garden? I want to scout for tracks," Lisa said, and there was a distinct bite to her tone.

"It rained last night," Henry said. "I doubt there will be much of his scent left."

"At least we can work out where he hid," Sam commented. "In case he decides to use the same spot again."

"He's clever." Lisa shoved at her irked feline, forcibly halting the beginnings of a shift. "He'll know we or the cops will check out these photos. He's taunting us. I cannot wait to catch this bastard and make him pay."

James Silcock's house

"What the devil do you think you're doing?" James demanded, going on attack as soon as he saw Tyler. His hands curled to fists at his side as he struggled with the urge to punch his brother in his arrogant Roman nose. "You pretended to be me at the advertising meeting. I told you I couldn't go. It was bad enough that you had to spread rumors and destroy her career and business, but now she thinks I had a part in pulling the plug on her reputation."

"The woman is a slut. She's living with three men—all younger. She deserves everything she gets."

The angry snarl on Tyler's lips gave James pause. His twin had become a stranger.

"I'm winning our game," Tyler said, his arrogance boosting the color in his cheeks.

"That's because I'm not playing any longer. You're out of line. It was meant to be fun. You weren't meant to destroy her reputation, her career."

"I didn't get where I am by acting like a pussy," Tyler sneered. "I give one hundred percent to every project I undertake. You're the same whiny, lily-livered boy that Mother always said you were."

James opened his mouth to defend himself then snapped it shut. He wouldn't dignify that with a reply. His conscience remained clear since he hadn't done anything more than ask her out on a date and drop around to deliver flowers after the Awards dinner. God, he still couldn't believe what Tyler had done to her, couldn't believe everyone believed her capable of such treachery. Shame filled him because it *was* he who had started this mess.

"You need to stop."

"No."

James stared at his brother. "This isn't funny. You're messing with her life. Hell, you're destroying it."

"No, this is research."

James felt his jaw drop, and he snapped his teeth together. "Do you always do such intense research?"

"Yes, how the devil do you think I manage to hit the bestseller lists? Why do you think my reviews always say how real my books feel?"

"I didn't think you took your research to these extremes," James snapped. A thought occurred. "Your last book was about a serial killer."

"Yes." Tyler met his gaze and didn't flinch.

But...but... God, Tyler wouldn't. He hadn't...surely?

"Did you hear the news?" Henry asked when Lisa and Sam arrived home from the supermarket.

Lisa dumped three bags of groceries on the counter. "No, we didn't have the radio on."

"James Silcock died in a motor vehicle accident this morning. The police aren't giving any details so far."

"What happened? Was another vehicle involved?" Lisa asked.

"He ran off the Coast Road and his vehicle plunged onto the rocks below."

"Hell," Sam said. "Now I feel guilty about maligning his character."

"He did try to steal your girl," Gerard said. "Any red-blooded man would get pissed at that."

"He was also one of the idiots who didn't give me a chance to defend my business reputation," Lisa said. "Even if he did try to apologize." She frowned. "I'm sorry he's dead though. I did like him at first."

"Our cop contact reckons your stalker is escalating. He told me to tell you to take extreme care when you go out and to lock all your doors when you're at home," Henry said.

"I can't be too careful or the bastard won't make a move."

Sam scowled. "We don't want to make it easy for him. One, he might get suspicious because he's aware you know you have a stalker and two, we don't want him to hurt you before we can nab him." He dragged his fingers through his black hair, leaving it sticking up in tufts. "I don't like this. My gut is singing a bad song."

Lisa went to him, and wrapped her arms around him. "We've discussed this, Sam. I—we—aren't going to have a normal life until we stop this guy. I think we should continue with our plan. We'll go out tonight and pretend it's a farewell dinner. Then I'll head home on my own and the three of you can come later to keep an eye on the place. It's a good plan. We've made it as safe as we can. I'll wear clothes that are easy to get out of, so I can shift. We'll take him by surprise. He won't be expecting a wolf and three big cats. If we scare him enough, he'll blubber to the cops and sound like a madman. It is a good plan," she insisted when Sam continued to look skeptical.

"Sam, my man," Gerard said. "We've discussed this."

Sam sighed and pulled away from Lisa. He started to pace. "I know, but put yourself in my position. How would you like it if your woman was the target?"

Gerard thumped him over the back. "I get it. I do. I'd feel the same way as you, but we have to stop this guy. The cops can't do anything, so we'll do their job for them."

Sam grumbled, but he stopped his arguing.

Lisa managed to design three more covers to place on her website. Although she hadn't received any orders yet, entries were pouring in for her competition. Hopefully, with a greater range of covers available someone would purchase one soon.

At six that evening, she packed up her laptop, happy with the amount of work she'd achieved.

She dressed in black for their big farewell dinner, in comfortable, slinky fabrics that stretched with ease. Although nerves lurked beneath the surface, determination kept her strong. She refused to keep living this way, scared and constantly looking over her shoulder.

Her stalker was going down.

"Talk about an anti-climax," Lisa said the next morning.

They'd met up at a newly renovated café, not far from the red zone—the area defined as too dangerous to enter after the big 'quake.

"I can't hang around," Sam said, pushing his empty plate away. "I have stuff I need to do."

"We'll watch Lisa today," Gerard promised.

"Make sure you do a good job. I'm trusting you with my girl. I'd better go."

"I'll wear a hat and glasses and different clothes," Henry said. "Pretend I'm a client. Expect me around ten."

"And I'll watch the area. Maybe do a jog past and check out things. We'll have our phones. You've entered our numbers on speed dial?"

Lisa grimaced. "You're a bunch of nanas. I have your numbers and I won't go anywhere, not even to the toilet, without my phone."

Sam checked his watch and stood. "I'd better go." He stooped to kiss Lisa. "I'll take care of the bill on the way out."

He left, and her feline rumbled out a complaint.

Gerard grinned. "Is he going to make an honest woman of you?"

"I might let him," she said.

"You're good for him." Henry pushed away from the table and stood. "I've never seen him serious about a woman before. Ten, okay? I won't look like me, so don't do anything rash."

Lisa drove home, and it was strange to be on her own after spending so much time with Sam and his friends. She missed Sam, which made her smile.

Be careful, sweetheart.

The soft sound of David's voice made her start as she pulled into her driveway. "Count on it."

You have a lot to live for now. Sam is perfect for you.

"Really? You're still matchmaking?"

You deserve the best.

"Thanks," she said, and with a deep breath, she climbed from her car. If only all this stalker business would go away, then she might start to enjoy her happiness.

She heard a faint bark from Geoffrey and several birds tweeted from the mature trees in the front of her garden, which told her no intruders skulked, ready to leap out at her. She cast out her senses and after smelling or seeing nothing out of place, she unlocked her house. Inside, she went through the same procedure. Listening. Scanning for anything out of place. Scenting the air.

Finally satisfied, she wandered to her kitchen to make a pot of tea. Mint tea today. In the kitchen and every room she entered, she went through her routine. Look. Listen. Scent. Sam would've been proud of her.

For two hours she worked. The doorbell went precisely at ten and she set down her pen and stood. At the door, she paused to do her checks, then cracked it open. A man in a suit stood there, a black leather briefcase in his left hand.

"Yes?"

"It's me," Henry said in a low voice and thrust out his hand.

Bemused, she took it and ushered him inside. "You scrub up well."

"I know," he said with a trace of arrogance. "I happen to prefer jeans."

Lisa laughed.

"See anything odd or out of place?"

Lisa shook her head. "Not a thing."

"Mrs. Humphries's dog is barking a lot."

"Yeah, he barked when I came home. Do you think I should go and check on her?"

"Wouldn't hurt. It's probably nothing. Any nibbles on your covers yet?"

"No, but it's early days. I need to get the word out."

"Have you tried Facebook yet?"

"Not yet."

"Why don't we join some author groups and do some advertising for half an hour or so? If he's watching, that's a reasonable amount of time for a meeting."

Lisa smiled. "That would be great! Maybe I can advertise my contest? I thought about trying some ads."

They worked together, chatting comfortably for almost an hour.

"I should go," Henry said.

"I'll show you out and go and see Mrs. Humphries," Lisa said.

At the door, she shook Henry's hand and smiled brightly, as if they'd concluded a successful business meeting. Her phone rang, and it was Gerard. She chatted about making an appointment. Henry climbed into his SUV and reached for his phone.

"Sam's idea," Gerard said. "Also, we thought it would drive your stalker crazy if he thinks you've managed to get your business going again."

"I'm heading over to Mrs. Humphries. Geoffrey hasn't stopped barking all morning."

"I'll see you soon."

"Thanks," Lisa said and hung up.

As she neared Mrs. Humphries's front door, the frenzied barks grew louder. Lisa frowned, then froze.

Blood. She smelled it the instant she stopped in front of the door. She swallowed and reached for the doorknob. The door wasn't locked.

Lisa picked up her phone to call Henry. "Something is wrong here. I can smell blood."

"Hang fire. I'm on my way."

While she waited, Lisa turned the knob and pushed the door open. Geoffrey sprinted out, growling at her on the run. His white coat bore streaks of blood, and the terrier left bloody footprints on the garden path.

"Mrs. Humphries?" she called as she edged through the door and hovered just inside.

There was no reply but along with the blood, she caught the scent of aftershave with a citrus aroma.

Her phone rang and she answered, not taking her gaze off the kitchen doorway in front of her.

"I've got Geoffrey," Henry said. "The cops are on the way. I'll let them come to the house instead of me. Do you think she's dead?"

"There's a lot of blood on Geoffrey. Do you think my stalker did this? I can smell his scent."

"I don't know. See what you can get from the cops."

"I can't hear anything. I might go inside—"

"No—"

Lisa hung up and called out again. "Mrs. Humphries? The police are coming." Although she could smell the stalker's aftershave, she thought he'd left. The dog would've behaved differently. Geoffrey had been barking when she arrived home. She took two more steps into the elderly woman's house and paused to scan the vicinity, then she noticed two legs on the kitchen floor. When she rounded the central granite counter, she found Mrs. Humphries lying on the floor, a pool of blood around her head.

Lisa knelt to check her pulse. The woman's body was already cold.

"Hands up," a male voice ordered from behind her.

Lisa complied as she stood. "I'm Lisa Jordan. I live next door. I got my friend to call you."

"You shouldn't be in here," the older of the two cops—a gray-haired man with thinning hair, black-rimmed glasses and a spare frame—said in clear disapproval.

"I haven't touched anything. All I did was check for a pulse."

"Stay there," the older cop ordered.

Lisa used the moment to scent the room. The stalker's scent filled the kitchen—not enough for a human to notice but she knew the man had spent time here.

"It looks as if she was surprised after she came home," the younger cop said. "Her wallet and everything else is still in her handbag. When did you see her last?"

"Yesterday. I saw her take her dog, Geoffrey, for a walk. I haven't seen her this morning."

"Where is her dog?" the older cop demanded.

"He ran out the door when I opened it. His coat was covered in blood." Lisa stopped, aware she'd started to chatter like a champion. She sucked in a quick breath in an attempt to regain her equilibrium. All along she'd thought this man—this stalker—a mere nuisance and a thorn in her side.

He was a murderer.

Mrs. Humphries might have put most nosy neighbors to shame, but she didn't deserve to die.

"Can I go home?"

"Which house do you live in?" the older cop asked.

"The white one next door."

He nodded. "We'll contact you if we have any further questions."

Lisa marched back to her house, the faint stinging at the back of her eyes telling her tears weren't far away.

James had died in the accident and now Mrs. Humphries was dead, murdered. A sob caught in her throat and she knuckled her eyes in an attempt to push back her emotion.

She needed to make sure she wasn't death number three for the week.

Chapter 11

The Trap and Love

Later that night.

L isa paced her kitchen, her feline so agitated that her skin twitched with the urgent need to shift. Every instinct she possessed told her the stalker would make his move tonight.

The cops had left Mrs. Humphries's house after interviewing her in depth as to her actions and activities this morning. They'd asked about her stalker since it became obvious Mrs. Humphries had notified the police of a man riding a motorbike hanging around their properties. She'd had to lie about part of her day, not wanting to land Henry or Gerard in trouble or to bring attention to them. She'd mentioned Sam and told them her boyfriend had farm chores, which was why she'd come home.

Her phone rang, and she jumped, letting out a feminine *eep* before her brain clicked into gear. Her feline made a *chuff-chuff* sound in her brain. Sly humor aimed at the human, frailer part of her psyche. Lisa's stomach did a loop-de-loop as she reached for her cell phone.

"Crap." This was harder than she'd imagined. "Yes?"

"I'm coming to get you," a singsong voice crooned.

Her hands turned clammy and her fingers gripped to the point of pain, then fury took over. "Who is this?"

"Gonna tie you up and tattoo your pretty skin. Everyone will know you belong to me."

She hung up. Immediately, the phone rang again. She hesitated then hit answer. "Listen here, you sicko. You can't go 'round making threats—"

"Lisa," a firm and familiar voice interrupted.

She gulped. "Oh, god. Sam. Sorry. He rang me, told me he was coming for me." She broke off to gasp in a breath. Her heart attempted to burrow from her chest, and she had to force herself to take slow, even breaths. She swallowed and started again. "He threatened to tattoo me."

"Lisa, listen to me. We're going to catch this cowardly bastard. *Lisa*. Breathe." Sam's calm voice helped to soothe her anxiety. "I rang to say we're in position. All four of us."

"Four?"

Sam laughed. "Yeah, Geoffrey refuses to leave Henry's side."

"He's mainly white. He'll shine like a beacon."

"We camouflaged him with mud."

"I bet he loved that."

Sam laughed. "He did. I don't think he's ever been allowed to get dirty."

"What about his growling? He's always growling at me."

"Henry fixed that too. He shifted to wolf and they barked and growled at each other. Henry seems to be able to get him to understand. He hasn't growled at Gerard or me since."

"Geoffrey is the strangest dog," Lisa said. And thanks to her conversation with Sam, most of her trepidation had settled. "I left the one window open a bit in the lounge, just as we planned. I opened all of my windows and made it look as if I forgot to shut one."

"All right. Get ready for bed and lock your bedroom door."

"We've discussed this. I'm not locking myself away. This creep has terrorized me for days. I want to bite his arse and scare the bejeepers out of him."

"Lock the door, Lisa."

Huh! Firm, alpha Sam making an appearance.

In the interest of expediency, she agreed.

"We're watching the house now. If you run into trouble, turn on your bedroom light."

"All right."

"I love you, Lisa. We're going to get this bastard."

"Okay. I guess I'd better get ready for bed." Not that she would sleep.

"See you soon," Sam said and hung up.

Lisa readied for bed, brushing her teeth and washing her face. She changed into a pair of pajamas and switched off her bedroom light, the last bit of illumination inside her house. At the last minute, she decided to shift to feline since she trusted her feline senses more than her human ones. She curled up in a ball and waited, praying fervently her stalker would make a move tonight. She couldn't take too many nights like this.

She must've drifted off to sleep because she woke without warning, a sense of wrongness assailing her.

The first of the stairs creaked, and instinct had her gliding off the bed and into the corner of the room. A faint light shone, and she realized her intruder possessed a torch to navigate her house. *Bastard*.

Every muscle in her body tensed as the rung near the top of the stairs creaked. She heard a pithy curse, voiced in an undertone, and watched the bob of the approaching light. It pierced the darkness of her bedroom and flitted across her empty bed.

"Oh, this will be fun. A cat and mouse game. Perfect for my book. I'll hit the bestseller lists for sure."

Lisa frowned at the familiar voice. That sounded like James, but that couldn't be right because he'd died in the accident. She slipped along the wall of her bedroom, knowing he wouldn't see her—not straightaway—because she blended with the shadows.

"Now where are you?" He stepped right into her bedroom and approached her bed. "Are you hiding?" He bent to shine his torch under her bed.

Lisa slipped out her bedroom door and waited just outside. Where were Sam and the others? They should have come by now. They would've seen him enter the window.

"Not under the bed," the man whispered. "Maybe you're hiding in the closet?"

Lisa froze. She needed a closer look at him. While she had no difficulty seeing him in the dark, he'd concealed his face. He sure sounded like James.

"I bet your heart is beating fast. You'll be trying to ring the cops without giving yourself away," he crooned. "Doesn't matter. I bet your hands are trembling so bad you're having trouble dialing."

He was right about her shaking. She couldn't seem to help herself. It was his voice. He sounded so confident and sure of himself. Heck, he seemed unconcerned about her calling the police, which told her he had a plan—maybe something they hadn't considered.

Lisa retreated, cursing inwardly. She'd left her phone sitting on the bedside cabinet.

"Oh, Lisa."

She halted at the top of the staircase on hearing the chiding note in his voice.

"You were so frightened you left your phone behind." He made a tsking sound at the back of his throat. "You'll be thinking that you'll use the land line, but that's not going to work. Should have grabbed your phone before you tried to hide from me, Lisa, babe. Aw, fuck. Didn't expect this to be so much fun. I've got a woody, Lisa. Might just need to rub it out in you."

Not in this lifetime.

The creak of the bottom rung on the stairs had him stilling.

"Ah, you've gone downstairs."

Backtracking, Lisa waited just outside her bedroom, glad help had arrived. She should have reminded Sam, Henry and Gerard about the creaks in the bottom and top stairs.

"You won't get outside before I grab you, Lisa. I've thought of everything."

His citrus aftershave assaulted her nostrils as he moved closer. She'd always liked a citrus scent. Not now. A shudder passed across her flanks.

"This game has been so much fun. Much better than last time," the man sing-songed. "Taking a life is powerful, but frightening you first upped the game so much. So heady. Addictive."

She didn't hear another creak, but caught Sam's welcome scent. The knowledge they were close brought confidence. She prowled toward the man, right into the searching beam of his small flashlight.

His shadowy bulk stiffened. "What the fuck?"

Who's frightened now? Bastard.

She rushed him, knocking him down with solid contact in the middle of his chest. He grunted as he struck the floor, winded by the force of her blow.

A small dark missile ran at them, a low bark rumbling through the darkness. Geoffrey. He seized the man's leg, and sank in his teeth. The man shrieked like a child having a tantrum.

"Get off. Get off me!" His arms flailed, but Geoffrey refused to release his grip. Another scream filled the landing.

Not so brave now. Lisa stood back and let Geoffrey have his moment.

"Seeing things. Not real. Not real. *Not real.*"

Lisa pushed her face close to the man's and tried not to breath in his stinky scent. Her whiskers twitched and she sneezed.

He screamed and screamed and screamed. Lisa drew back with feline hauteur.

"You all right, Lisa?" Gerard's voice.

She issued a feline snarl.

"I'll ring the cops."

The man screamed again, and Lisa smelled blood. Geoffrey attacked the man's arm and she let him, doing nothing to stop the determined dog. He deserved revenge as much as she did.

A feral growl came from behind her. The man moaned, his scream cut off abruptly.

Lisa cuffed the man across the face with her paw and dislodged his mask. Once. Twice, before Sam nudged her insistently.

He was right to interrupt. She needed to shift and dress before the cops arrived.

She retreated to her bedroom and shifted. After pulling on her discarded pajamas, she switched on the light then the one on the landing.

Her gaze went to the man. He writhed on the floor with Henry standing over him in wolf form. Geoffrey stood beside Henry, vibrating with the intensity of his growls.

"Not real. Not real." The man shook his head from side to side. "Not real. *Not real!*"

Sam padded toward her and rubbed against her legs before he disappeared in the direction of one of the spare bedrooms. Minutes later, he returned fully dressed and Henry took a turn to shift and dress in the clothes he'd left in her spare bedroom earlier, Geoffrey trailing after him.

"Do you know him?" Sam frowned at the man on the floor.

"It's James. I don't understand," she said, staring at him while confusion pushed a scowl onto her face.

"I'll go and wait for the cops," Gerard said.

Henry and Geoffrey approached them, and the dog charged the man again, sinking his teeth into the man's arm before Henry barked a stern order at him. Geoffrey retreated with obvious reluctance.

"Cops are here," Gerard called out. "Everyone decent?"

"Yes." Lisa crouched beside the weeping man. "What book are you talking about?"

"My book, you stupid bitch." James regained his courage. "My fuckin' book."

Geoffrey snarled and the man flinched, losing his bravado. Lisa growled at him, letting her feline shine through her eyes.

The man whimpered and attempted to shrink into the carpet as she lowered her face to his. "What are you?"

"Not a woman to mess with," she hissed at him.

He wrenched something from his pocket, and she slapped it away on instinct. The syringe flew from his grasp.

"He intended to drug me," she said, her gaze on the device.

Low voices came from her front door. The cops. She straightened.

"He had a key," Gerard told the two cops when they reached the top of the flight of stairs.

He did? Lisa scowled. She had all her keys. She would've missed them. No, wait... David's keys. She'd left them in her desk drawer. Rats, she hadn't even missed them.

"I keep a spare set in my desk drawer. I didn't even realize they were missing," Lisa said.

"Do you recognize him?" Detective Fisher, their police contact, asked. He produced a plastic baggie and reached for the syringe with a gloved hand, placing it inside.

Lisa frowned. "It's James Silcock, but I don't understand. He was reported dead—the coastal accident, mentioned on the news a couple of days ago."

The detective shared a glance with his partner. "James Silcock did die in the accident this week. Positive identification. We've kept this quiet, but his brake line was cut."

"Murder?" Lisa whispered. "I still don't understand. Who is this?"

"I believe this is Tyler Silcock, James's identical twin. We weren't aware of his existence until we started digging deeper. We noticed someone was using the spare bedroom at James's house. There were two sets of dishes in the kitchen sink, which made us curious."

"These people are crazy." Tyler pushed to his feet, projecting a confident persona for the police. Lisa witnessed the slyness return to his expression. Scary and freaky watching him in action. "I want to press charges. They let their dogs attack me. And the cats. Officer, I wish to press charges. But first, you will take me to the hospital. I could have rabies."

Geoffrey growled and darted at Tyler.

Tyler let out an embarrassing shriek and attempted to hide behind the nearest policeman. Two policemen in uniform walked up the stairs and waited quietly for orders.

"Handcuff him and take him to the station," Detective Fisher instructed.

"Did you hear me?" Tyler shouted. "I want to press charges. I might have rabies."

Lisa frowned at him. "What are you talking about? I don't own any cats." Her acting skills were excellent.

Henry turned to one of the cops. "Maybe he's been taking drugs. He's said a few weird things about books and cats and research."

"I am a bestselling author," Tyler snapped. "I want to call my lawyer."

One of the policemen placed handcuffs on him. "You can phone him from the police station." He led Tyler down the stairs and another officer escorted him in the rear.

"Is there somewhere we can sit to take your statements?" Detective Fisher asked.

Lisa worked to suppress her sigh. More acting required. She forced a smile. "How about the kitchen, then I can make everyone coffee or tea if you prefer."

"That sounds perfect," Detective Fisher said. "Lead the way."

The next morning, after minimal sleep, Lisa entered her bedroom to pack a bag. She couldn't stay here. Not any longer.

Sell the place, sweetheart. If you stay here, you'll have nightmares about Mrs. Humphries and you couldn't spend the night in this room because of him. Go and live with your Sam. You love him.

"You don't mind?" Lisa whispered as she tossed underwear and warm jumpers into her suitcase.

You love Sam. I know it. You know it. It's time for you to tell Sam and step boldly into the future.

Lisa considered David's words and nodded. Their courtship hadn't exactly been traditional, but it had been the same with her marriage to David. She'd never regretted her decision. Her and Sam—it felt the same. Perfect. *Right.*

You deserve happiness, sweetheart. That is what I wish for you.

"Okay," she whispered, smiling as she packed. David had confirmed her thoughts. She'd fallen well and truly for Sam.

"We should go for a run," Sam said later that evening. Lisa had just finished speaking with Detective Fisher on the phone. All the chores were done and darkness shrouded the countryside, the days shorter now that winter approached. "Just a quick one. I need to get rid of some surplus energy after last night. My feline wanted to rip into that man for scaring you."

Lisa nodded. "I'd love to run out some frustration. I wanted to take a chunk out of him for Mrs. Humphries. I'm glad they were able to tie him to her murder. She might have been nosy and a gossip, but no one deserves to die that way. At least Geoffrey got in a few shots on her behalf, and we have the satisfaction of knowing the creep will be locked up. Detective Fisher told me he kept detailed notes of his activities. *A diary of my reactions.* He's responsible for my loss of reputation, the bastard."

"Once his activities become public knowledge, your name will be cleared."

"Not quick enough. You know they found other diaries he'd written earlier. Detective Fisher is passing the info to American authorities since they detail murders in Las Vegas."

"Yeah, Henry mentioned the diaries when he rang. He was pissed because he thought the murder charges would push Silcock's book sales."

Lisa pulled a face. "He won't enjoy the financial gain. Detective Fisher thinks he killed the women for research for his novel."

"Sick fuck. You had a lucky escape."

"They suspect he murdered his brother too, although he's refusing to discuss James. He kept mentioning his book and how he intended to hit the New York Times bestseller lists. I heard the cops discussing him, how he showed no remorse. He's sick all right." A shiver frisked her as she thought of poor Mrs. Humphries, of James. "I want to put Tyler Silcock out of my mind. They've caught him, and that is the important thing. According to Detective Fisher, none of his fancy lawyers will get him off the murder and stalking charges. I'm happy with that and will do my part."

Sam reached for her hand and squeezed. "Let's go then. A quick run then we'll come back here for shower sex. After that, we can hit the bedroom for round two."

They grabbed coats, and Lisa let Sam lead her outside onto the deck. She grinned at him as they pulled on gumboots. "Great thinking." She rather enjoyed the way her new bright red gumboots looked beside Sam's plain black ones.

Clouds obscured most of the moon and a morepork, a New Zealand native owl, hooted three times. After seconds of silence in which she heard nothing but the crunch of gravel beneath their feet, another morepork answered from a nearby stand of trees. Sam laced his fingers with hers as they strode into the darkness. Out here in the countryside, and away from the house, the stars shone brightly and the air smelled cleaner. The angst she'd worn, like an extra layer of clothing had dispersed. There was a spring in her step while she reveled being with Sam.

She dragged in a deep lungful of clean air and caught a hint of horse from a neighboring paddock. "It's beautiful out here."

"It is." Sam's eyes glowed, but they didn't take in the scenery or the night sky with the stars peeking through the cloud gaps. No, he was looking at her, and it struck her anew, this feeling that she needed him, didn't want to live without him in her life.

"I love you, Sam," she whispered.

He gripped her shoulders, dragging her close. His chest heaved as if he'd run a race, and he nuzzled her loose hair before pushing her away to study her face. Male arrogance surfaced in him, finding an outlet in a smirk. "About time."

Lisa laughed, her amusement ending with a shriek when he seized her in his arms. With her help, he opened and closed a gate and strode to a grassy area, screened from the driveway by a hedge.

Lisa peered into the dark. "Are there animals in this paddock?"

Sam huffed out a laugh and set her on her feet. "No, although there will be tomorrow."

He dragged off his long jacket, draped it on a grassy patch, and their lips met in an urgent kiss. Her brain short-circuited under his raw and primal kisses, and all she could do was hang on for the ride. His cock swelled between them and an answering arousal throbbed through her pussy, her flesh dampening in preparation for their joining. When they parted, they both breathed like runners finishing a race.

"Strip," he ordered in a husky voice.

Something inside her softened, then jumped in anticipation. She loved him. Somehow, she'd lucked out and found a man who completed her, who made her feel whole yet never stifled her independence. She dragged off her boots, her clothes, wanting to join with him so badly she ached. When her last bit of clothing hit the ground, a laugh erupted. "Hope we can find them in the dark. Even with feline eyesight, it's dark out tonight."

"We'll find them."

"We will. I'm not facing your staff tomorrow morning and answering embarrassing questions."

"We could always tell them we're going to start a bra fence or a boot fence."

"Pardon?"

Sam's grin appeared white and happy in the faint light. "They have a few farther south. Women have draped their bras on a farmer's fence. There are all shapes and sizes from sexy to granny. Another farmer has a fence covered with shoes."

Lisa sniffed while trying to contain the giddy happiness attempting to burst free. "You are not hanging my bra on a fence, although maybe the Feline Council might like to try that in Middlemarch. You could tell your cousin Saber. Isn't he on the council?"

"He is and that's a great idea. Saber could use a fence in an area where none of the shifters are likely to want to run. I'll suggest it next time I talk to him, but meantime..." He licked the tender skin behind her ear, the extreme roughness of his tongue telling her how close his feline hovered to the surface. "Tell me again," he demanded.

She knew exactly what he wanted. "I love you."

"Damn, Lisa. I never thought I'd hear you say those words. I'm crazy about you. I want you for my mate, to share my life and have children with you." He lifted her off her feet and placed her on his jacket, dropping to the ground at her side.

"Yes," she agreed, pressing closer. She didn't have the slightest doubt. "I've decided to sell my house. I'm hoping you'll let me live with you."

He pressed a kiss to her lips, which ignited and burned out of control. Long seconds later, he dragged his mouth off hers and stared down at her. "Can I take you from behind?"

An unasked question lurked in his words, but she never hesitated. "Take me. I'm all yours."

Sam flipped her over, stroking her buttocks and tugging her nipples in the manner she enjoyed. She shivered beneath his caresses, parting her legs under his guidance. One big hand pushed aside the fall of her hair so he could nuzzle her neck, his ragged breathing hinting at his urgency.

"Sam." Her voice held both yearning and need. She was fine with the fast pace, because now that she'd made her decision, made peace with her lingering guilt and David, she accepted the truth of her and Sam.

"Steady, sweetheart. There's no need to hurry."

A frustrated groan escaped her and Sam's laugh rang out. His tongue darted across her marking spot before he withdrew to tease the whorls of her ear.

Lisa snatched a hasty breath, her skin incredibly sensitive beneath his searching tongue. "I think you're wrong. I want you to fuck me, bite me, take me in all ways. Right now."

The play of his fingers, the way his tongue teased her made her belly clench, her nerve endings sizzle with impatience. He was going to send her mad. She turned her head to glower at him and he laughed again.

Sam continued at his own pace, feathering kisses down her throat, making teasing forays over her marking site. The breeze cooled her skin while a bird in a tree to their left hooted at them, indignant at their trespassing. Beneath her hands and knees, crushed grass let off a distinctive fresh, green scent. The next time she smelled trampled grass, she'd think of this moment, recall the way he touched her and the care and love that came with each of his caresses. Love swelled inside her for this special man.

He crowded her, covering her with his larger frame while his fingers tested her readiness. A harsh growl of pleasure emerged from her when he pushed into her, his cock stretching her silken walls. Fiery sensation flared in her pussy, her pulse skittering while the rich scent of arousal swirled around them. He started to shaft her deeply. She pushed back, trembling because she was so close.

Sam grunted and shoved into her, his teeth fastening on the fleshy pad of skin where shoulder and neck met. Pain streaked through her, followed by a contrasting shard of pleasure that made her cry out. She went liquid deep inside, the hum of pleasure building with each decisive push of his shaft. Tension spiked, the rasp of his tongue across her marking spot and the urgent tempo of his cock too much to bear. She shattered, pulsing around his shaft, ecstasy striking her hard. Strangled gasps tore from her throat as she sobbed out her pleasure.

Sam pulled back and pounded into her again, groaning. His big body shook as climax took him, his teeth still gripping her. When the spasms eased, Sam released his grasp. He lapped his tongue over the wound to allow the enzymes in their blood to mingle and the mark to heal.

Long minutes later, he separated their bodies and turned her to face him. There was no mistaking the smug grin of triumph in her new mate. She couldn't help her rueful smile in return and the wave of love so big she wondered if she could contain the emotion.

I told you he loves you. The two of you are good together. It's time for me to leave.

David?

I'll always love you, but now you have Sam. He's a worthy mate. My work here is done.

David? He didn't answer, and Lisa suspected he'd gone for good this time. But instead of an aching emptiness, she felt acceptance. Love.

She wound her arms around Sam's neck and pressed her lips against his to redirect some of his smugness. "You. Me. A bed. Very soon," she said when their lips parted. "By tomorrow morning you're gonna wear a matching mark."

"I can't wait. I love you, Lisa."

She thought she saw the sheen of emotional tears in his beautiful eyes, and everything inside her squeezed in response.

Lisa released a rumbling purr and smiled, accepting his love with openness and belief. Sam Mitchell was her mate, and she was the happiest feline female alive.

Want a hint about what comes next? Remember when Sam and Lisa left the Middlemarch Singles Ball, and Sam spotted his cousin Saber with a mystery woman? If you haven't already read My Scarlet Woman, this is

Saber's story. If you have read this one—fantastic! Felix, Saber's brother and Sam's cousin, finds his love next in My Peeping Tom. Meantime, read on for a special bonus chapter featuring a Feline Council meeting.

Chapter 12

Bonus: Shifter Meeting

F eline Shapeshifter Council Meeting, Saber Mitchell's house, Middlemarch

Present: Saber Mitchell, Sid Blackburn, Kenneth Nesbitt, Agnes Paisley, Valerie McClintock, Benjamin Urquart

The scent of lemon furniture polish filled the air. A fire crackled in the hearth and a white vase filled with red flowers sat on the coffee table. The stack of farming magazines was no longer visible, placed in the study at Emily's behest. Saber smiled as he waited for the council members to arrive for the meeting. His younger brothers grumbled about the changes around the house, and the fact they had to keep the kitchen, dining room and lounge free of clutter, but he didn't think they minded having Emily living with them. She certainly made him happy.

The phone rang and Saber picked it up. "Hey, Sam." He listened to his cousin, heard the joy in his voice. "That's great. Congratulations. Give Lisa a kiss for me." He laughed at Sam's possessive growl and totally understood his cousin's position. Anyone kissing Emily took their life in their hands. They chatted about the price of beef. "An idea? Sure. A bra fence?" A chuckle escaped. "Not sure Agnes and Valerie will approve of that. A shoe fence? I'll give them your suggestions. Come to visit soon. You can meet Emily. Some shifter friends? Sure, bring them out. Yeah okay. See you soon."

He hung up with a grin. One thing his brothers never complained about was the improved food. Casseroles, full of chunks of beef—like the one currently cooking in the crockpot while Emily catered for Katy Urquart's birthday party at Storm in a Teacup—had become the norm. Emily was a better cook than any of them.

A tap at the door rippled through the air, followed by a hearty, "Saber, lad, are you there?"

Saber strode to answer the summons and ushered Sid and Kenneth in from the cold. No snow yet, but the nip in the air foretold a chilly winter.

"Agnes and Valerie won't be long. They're coming with Benjamin," Sid said. "Something smells good."

"Emily put on a casserole before she left to take care of Katy's party." Saber shut the door and followed the men into the dining room where they customarily held their meetings. Usually monthly, but recently, given all the organization and changes they wanted to make for the community, the meetings had become weekly.

A brown cloth covered the table and a stack of plates and cups stood ready. Emily had placed a centerpiece in the middle—an arrangement of miniature pink roses and some greenery. She'd also hunted out notepaper plus a stack of pens in case they wanted to take notes.

"Smells good." Kenneth nodded. "But there's more. Your house smells like family, looks like family, feels like family." A smile of satisfaction wreathed his beefy face.

"I'll start the coffee." Saber left the two shifters in the dining room and strode into the kitchen. Kenneth was right. Emily's presence, her love, had shaped them into a family. He glanced at his watch and restrained a groan with difficulty. Hours until she returned. Hours before he could kiss her, touch her. *Hours.*

A thump on the door raised a grimace. Ben and the women had arrived. He'd bet it was Valerie thumping for entrance. The woman possessed not a scrap of patience, unless she went to the school to fill in for one of the teachers.

"I'll get it," Sid called out.

Saber grabbed the plate of pikelets and another of bacon and egg savories Emily had made for their meeting and carried them to the dining room. "Coffee won't be long."

Valerie strode up to him and gave him a hug. Saber froze as a wave of lavender and feline engulfed him, shock doing a number on his vocal chords. Who was this woman? Certainly not the Valerie McClintock of his experience.

She pulled away and patted his hand. "You're a good lad. I'm so pleased you and Emily are getting married."

"When is the wedding?" Agnes took her place, and this time, he got a dose of feline, mint and lemon laundry powder as the woman hugged him. "You've done well, Saber. We're proud of you."

"We're going to grab a week in October and go to Fiji. Emily didn't want a splashy ceremony since we're already mates and she's done it before. We'll formalize our marriage there."

"Congratulations on finding your mate," Ben said.

Sid nodded. "If you don't treat Emily right, I'll steal her away from you. Herbert would have liked her."

Ken cackled from his seat at the table. "Better shut your mouth, lad, before an insect mistakes it for an invitation."

"You can't get married without us," Valerie protested.

"We are getting married in Fiji. It's what Emily wants."

"The lad is entitled to do things his own way," Sid said, staring at each of his friends in turn. Saber hoped Sid's silent rebuke worked but didn't hold much hope.

"You don't like flying," Kenneth said.

"I will do it for Emily."

Agnes scowled at him, then brightened. "We'll have a party on your return then. Can we do that? A party for the shifter community?"

Fuck, they were a determined, stubborn lot. His shoulders slumped as he admitted defeat. "We'd like that."

"Excellent." Valerie rubbed her hands together and beamed at him. "When are you planning on starting a family?"

Really? Saber pressed his lips together, scanned their expectant faces and shook his head. "I'll get the coffee." He escaped to the kitchen and pinched himself. Yep, he was awake all right. He carried out the coffeepot and a jug of milk.

"Where are your brothers today?" Agnes asked once he'd set the items on the table. "These look good. Are they bacon and egg?"

"Yes." He took a breath to marshal his thoughts and his patience. He wasn't sure what his brothers were doing today, apart from Leo. "Emily made them."

"Leo is helping Emily at Katy's birthday party." Ben chuckled. "I saw him dressed as a prince. Katy and her friends are enjoying it, but I'm not so sure about Leo."

"Emily bribed him with his favorite dinner," Saber said, grinning at the memory of his bemused brother. "He'd agreed before he knew what struck him."

Valerie arranged the cups and gestured Saber for the coffeepot. Wary, he sank onto his chair and waited for normality to return.

"Right," said Sid, once they'd organized food and coffee. "What is next on our to-do list?"

"Sam rang me a few minutes ago," Saber said. "He's mated with Lisa Jordan. He suggested we start a shoe fence or a bra fence to attract tourists. Put it in a place away from where we might run."

"Not a bra fence. That is not the impression we want to set for Middlemarch," Valerie stated.

Sid nodded. "Thought of that myself. We could have a padlock fence. Sell padlocks at all the stores in the town, along with a map to the fence. Something to signify romance."

"Now that is a good idea," Saber said. "We should do the padlocks. The funds from the sale of the padlocks can help with our latest community project."

Valerie added a spoon of sugar to her coffee. "That is an excellent idea. Should we vote?"

"I think everyone is in favor," Ben said, glancing around the table.

"Done," Sid said. "What next?"

"That pesky reporter is hanging around still." Kenneth shared his irritation around the table, his scowl dark and powerful. "Greg says she's signed a lease for six months. She's still asking questions. She cornered me in the café the other day. Wanted to know about the panther sightings."

"Humph," Valerie said. "We're leopards, not panthers."

Ben tapped his fingers on the table. "If no one is talking to her, what can she do? She'll get sick of it soon and give up."

"We need to reiterate to the youngsters that they mustn't shift without checking the vicinity for humans first," Agnes said.

Ah, Agnes was giving him the look, an accusation directed to his brothers.

"I've already told them," Saber replied. "And I delivered the same lecture to each of their friends. They're taking care."

"All right," Sid said. "If each of us pass the message on to our families, that will help. What else? Should we get to work on the sports fields?"

"We'll need to do some fundraising first," Ben said. "Maybe another dance, but just for those who live locally."

Valerie sipped her coffee and helped herself to a pikelet. She took a bite, leaving a hint of cream on her top lip. "What about holding the dance at the old historic shearing shed on Sid's property? It'd need sprucing up, but would it work as a venue? Sid?"

"That's a good idea. There is plenty of parking," Kenneth said. "But how is that going to help our young males find mates. Everyone will know each other."

"It's not good to go about the matchmaking in a blatant manner," Saber said. "My brothers, for one, will dig in their heels if they think I'm trying to manage their love lives." He paused to eye each of the council members. "That includes me."

"I thought it turned out rather well," Sid said with a smile. "It is excellent news about your cousin and Lisa."

Agnes lifted her coffee cup in salute. "The Mitchell men are falling like flies."

"Back to the sports field," Saber said firmly. "I think we should make a field near the school so they can use the facilities, but a more private one, just for shifters, might make sense. That way we can play rugby or volleyball or soccer in either form. We can use the area for picnics during the summer and not worry too much about humans seeing us when they shouldn't. Perhaps someone could donate a spot? We'd need room for private parking too."

Ben nodded, his fingers tap-tap-tapping the tabletop again. "I like the idea of a private field. Anyone have any suggestions as to location?"

"We'd need flat land," Kenneth said.

"Our place might work," Agnes said. "I'll need to discuss it with my son, but we have flat land out the back of our farm. Everyone would need to park at the rear of our house, behind the barn and walk up the track to the flats. The downside is that it's grazing land."

Ben reached for a savory and placed it on his plate. "What if we charged a gold coin admission fee every time we used the field or a bale of hay? That way Agnes's son is receiving hay or money to buy feed, yet the fee is affordable for all of us."

Agnes leaned back in her chair, nodding with decisiveness. "I think Brian would go for that. After all, he could still graze the area with his stock between gatherings. We can all have a good run, and it will be something for the children and younger felines to do."

"So, we're decided on our next projects. We organize the padlock fence, the woolshed dance and get the sports fields underway. The ones at the school will need to be done properly because we'll have visiting sports teams, but the private fields can be more informal. They'll require mowing when we want to use them." Sid glanced at each of them for approval.

"I like all the ideas," Saber said. "I'll take charge of organizing the fields at the school. We have the empty lot there, which was always intended for that purpose."

"Agnes and I can take care of the food for the woolshed dance," Valerie said. "Everyone can bring a plate. That will make it simple."

"I'll organize the drinks," Kenneth said. "We made a healthy profit at our first dance. Some of that money can go toward the expenses for the new sportsgrounds."

"Ben and I will organize the shed and the band," Sid suggested. "How about a gold coin admission fee there too? We'll send out word in the local newsletter and put up a notice at the pub, the café and the store."

"Wonderful," Agnes said as she reached for a pikelet. "Your Emily is a talented cook."

"She is." A sound distracted Saber, the purr of a familiar vehicle, the slam of a door. Emily was home early. Pleasure flooded him. They'd have the house to themselves, once he ended the meeting and got rid of this nosy lot.

The front door opened and closed, and Saber stood. He ignored the stirring around the table and went to meet his mate.

"You're home early."

"Everything is under control, so I decided to finish for the day. How is the meeting?"

"Emily," Valerie called. "Come and have a cup of coffee with us."

Unable to help himself, Saber reached for his mate's hand. He twined their fingers together, her touch bringing a rush of joy and contentment. He led her to the dining room.

"We've almost finished," he said and communicated his determination with each of the council members by giving them *the look*.

They, of course, ignored him.

Emily smiled. "Just a quick cup of coffee. I need to make a birthday cake for a party early next week, and I wanted to do a trial run."

To Saber's frustration, the council members settled in for a good natter. Finally, half an hour later, he stood. "It is time for you to leave. Will we meet at the same time next week?"

"Saber," Emily said, her cheeks going pink.

"No, the lad is right. We've teased him long enough." Sid stood. "Thank you for the afternoon tea, Emily. The pikelets were delicious."

"I can tell you're going to become invaluable to our community," Agnes said.

To Saber's astonishment Agnes hugged Emily then gave him the same treatment. His mouth dropped open as Valerie embraced them both too.

Ben was next. He kissed Emily on the cheek and shook Saber's hand. He winked and leaned closer to say, "Hell does freeze over sometimes."

"Thank you, lad," Sid said. "We'll see you next week."

The house cleared and the vehicles departed. Saber turned to Emily and reclaimed her hand. He tugged her toward him, his feline letting out a little purr of satisfaction. "Alone at last." He cupped her cheek and met her smiling gaze. "What should we do?"

Author Note

S o we've come to an end, but we're not finished yet! You have three assignments before we part ways.

Join my newsletter.

My author newsletter is full of fun stuff, including news of upcoming books, bargains, cover reveals, contests, and more. Sign up today and receive a copy of the prequel to the Middlemarch Shifters series.

Enjoyed My Younger Lover?

Reviews are so important for indie authors like me who don't have the backing of a large publishing house. Please post a review and share what you liked or didn't like.

Read more books in the Middlemarch Shifters World

There are 16 books in the Middlemarch Shifters series, plus I have two spin-off series—Middlemarch Capture and Middlemarch Gathering. And best of all, while the stories are set in the same world, they're all stand-alone romances. No cliffhangers here! Read them in any order.

Middlemarch Shifters
Middlemarch Capture
Middlemarch Gathering

Until next time. Happy reading!

Shelley

About Author

USA Today bestselling author Shelley Munro lives in Auckland, the City of Sails, with her husband and a cheeky Jack Russell/mystery breed dog.

Typical New Zealanders, Shelley and her husband left home for their big OE soon after they married (translation of New Zealand speak - big overseas experience). A twelve-month-long adventure lengthened to six years of roaming the world. Enduring memories include being almost sat on by a mountain gorilla in Rwanda, lazing on white sandy beaches in India, whale watching in Alaska, searching for leprechauns in Ireland, and dealing with ghosts in an English pub.

While travel is still a big attraction, these days Shelley is most likely found in front of her computer following another love - that of writing stories of contemporary and paranormal romance and adventure. Other interests include watching rugby (strictly for research purposes), cycling, playing croquet and the ukelele, and curling up with an enjoyable book.

Visit Shelley at her Website
www.shelleymunro.com

Join Shelley's Newsletter
www.shelleymunro.com/newsletter

Visit Shelley's Facebook page
www.facebook.com/ShelleyMunroAuthor

Follow Shelley at Bookbub
www.bookbub.com/authors/shelley-munro

Also By Shelley

SHELLEY MUNRO

My Blue Lady
My Twin Trouble
My Precious Gift

Middlemarch Gathering
My Highland Mate
My Highland Fling

Middlemarch Capture
Snared by Saber
Favored by Felix
Lost with Leo
Spellbound with Sly
Journey with Joe
Star-Crossed with Scarlett